I0661918

James Butler

Fortune's Foot Ball or The Adventures of Mercutio - Founded on Matters of Fact

Vol. II

James Butler

Fortune's Foot Ball or The Adventures of Mercutio - Founded on Matters of Fact
Vol. II

ISBN/EAN: 9783337064297

Printed in Europe, USA, Canada, Australia, Japan

Cover: Foto ©Andreas Hilbeck / pixelio.de

More available books at **www.hansebooks.com**

OR, THE

ADVENTURES

OF

MERCUTIO.

FOUNDED ON MATTERS OF FACT.

A NOVEL, IN TWO VOLUMES.

BY JAMES BUTLER.

VOL. II.

HARRISBURGH, PENNSYLVANIA:
PRINTED BY JOHN WYETH

1768.

[ENTERED ACCORDING TO LAW.]

FORTUNE's FOOT-BALL.

"NOTHING could have increafed the agitation of my mind during the remainder of that day: Several times I was tempted to accufe my kind keeper of infidelity; again I would reproach myfelf with injuftice and in-gratitude—In the midft of my reveries the door of my cell flew open, and the keeper beckoned me to fol-low him: I obeyed without fpeaking a word—He led me to the outer gate, where ftood the Friar.—He unlocked the gate and we fallied forth precipitately.—We went through a narrow ftreet which led to the open country.

"After we had travelled about two miles, at a pret-ty round rate, he led us into a wood, and defired us to wait his return in filence. We retired about a hun-dred yards into the wood and fat down; the Friar be-gan to return thanks for fo fuccefsful a beginning, in which I joined him, and, after fome preparatory dif-courfe, he informed me that they defigned to go to Le-on, where he had a brother fuperior of a Monaftery. He then very kindly inftructed me how to conduct my-felf; pointing out the neareft and moft private ways to

Leghorn, where, he obferved, I might probably meet with a veffel bound to fome port in Great-Britain.

" Our companion then appeared riding one horfe, and leading two others faddled: We mounted and rode together about ten Englifh miles, and then halted exactly in the interfection of two roads, where we took an affectionate leave of each other : They proceeded ftraight forward ; and I, agreeably to the directions of my fellow travellers, took the right hand road.

" Having travelled through moft parts of Italy in my youthful days, I was not much at a lofs ; but found the way to Leghorn very readily, where I difpofed of the horfe to great advantage. Thus, gentlemen and ladies, I have given you a fuccinct account of all the difafters which has befel me fince I parted with my pupil here ; and I affure you I look on my efcape as very little fhort of a miracle."

They all heartily congratulated him on his good fortune, and, having a fine leading wind and pleafant weather, they fpent their time very agreeably, until they had paffed the Iflands of Majorca and Minorca, and were in expectation of running the ftreights of Gibraltar without danger or difficulty.

Our hero was, at that period, as happy as he had ever been ; he enjoyed the higheft felicity in the vivifying converfation of the charming Ifabella; and agreeable company of his fellow voyagers : Certain it is, that in this small society, composed as it was of persons of different ages, sexes, countries and religious denominations, there reigned what is rarely, if ever, found in the levees of the most august princes, namely, sincerity : Freedom of sentiment was attended to without censure or disgust ; difference of opinions produced neither ceremony nor contempt ; convivial harmony reverberated from breast to breast, and it was the delight of each to contribute to the satisfaction of the other.

Thus situated, with the firmest confidence of landing safely in his native country in a short space, is it a wonder that the mind of Mercutio was tranquil, and that his rising hopes destroyed the conception of disappointment?—This was the case.

But fortune, that fickle goddess, who delights in tantalizing her votaries, and in sporting with their sensibility, withdrew her amiable smiles, determined to give him one more kick, lest he should suppose himself out of the reach of her heel. They had just lost sight of Majorca when a violent hurricane overtook them, which threw the whole company into the utmost consternation. The captain gave orders for furling the sails with all the expedition possible; in the mean time, he was obliged to assist at the helm which the violence of the tempest rendered indispensible necessary. In the midst of this dreadful conflict between the contending elements, a sudden and tremendous squall deprived the ship of her main-top-maſt, together with ſix of her ableſt ſeamen, who were, unfortunately, on the main-top-ſail-yard, furling the top-ſail.

This was a dreadful ſtroke, of which the captain was fully ſenſible; however, he continued to give his orders with compoſure and firmneſs; and was obeyed by his men with intrepidity and alacrity. The ſtorm raged ſixteen hours, without intermiſſion or abatement, and was ſucceeded by dark, cloudy weather, and a briſk gale of wind for ſeveral days. Every other perſon on board appeared more concerned for their perſonal ſafety than Mercutio, who had, by a long ſeries of misfortunes, diſappointments and dangers, become habituated to them; he had acquired an uniformity of temper and a ſerenity of countenance on all occaſions, which amazed his companions, and was peculiar to himſelf: He diſplayed, however, on this occaſion, a more than ordinary degree of compoſure, which was abſolutely neceſſary, to inſpire Iſabella with fortitude to ſupport her in that alarming ſituation.

Early one morning they were again overtaken by a moſt tremendous hurricane; heavy ſqualls of hail, accompanied with dreadful claps of thunder and almoſt inceſſant ſtreams of lightning, continued to annoy them until ſeven in the evening, when the clouds began to diſperſe; but a heavy weſtern gale continued to blow with unabating rigour, for the ſpace of four days and nights. Their fortitude entirely forſook them! Even

Mercutio had nearly forbore to hope! The sea rolled in dreadful mountains, so that, considering the shattered condition of the ship, and the loss of the six men, it was little less than a miracle that they were not entombed in the ocean.

At length it pleased God to lull the furious waves into a state of perfect tranquillity; and the surface of the capacious bed of waters, smooth and transparent, once more met their ravished sight. Soothing as this change certainly was; yet very serious apprehensions began to arise in their minds, when the captain on taking observation, informed them that they were then within sixty leagues of Candia, a large island in the Mediterranean, belonging to the grand Signior, a noted resort for Pirates.

They consulted on the most expedient and prompt measures to adopt, for their preservaion. It was observed by the captain, that should they be attacked by any of those inhuman pirates which infest the Mediterranean, they must inevitably fall victims to their cruelty; as they were destitute of the means of defence or flight, and he therefore gave it as his opinion, that as the ship was much disabled, it would be best to endeavour to make the island of Sicily, where they might refit, take in fresh provision and water, and refresh themselves in the mean time.

This proposal met the approbation of the whole company; in consequence of which, the captain gave orders to tack, intending to put into Messina. Though the wind was on the beam, yet they entertained the most sanguine hopes of obtaining the desired object, notwithstanding their speed was much retarded by the craziness of the vessel, which leaked considerably. They stood on this course from half past eight in the morning until evening, and though with all the industry they were able to exert, they could gain but two knots and a half per hour, yet were in tolerable spirits. The horizon had intercepted about half the beauties of the sun when they discovered a vessel bearing after them under all her canvas. When this news was first communicated to the captain he appeared somewhat embarrassed; however, he encouraged his company with hopes of its being an English ship from the Levant, homeward bound. Notwithstanding these hopes, he crouded all the sail his ship would bear, and bore away for the streights of Messina.

The darkness of the night prevented the captain from seeing his pursuers, though he remained on deck all night for that purpose; but he perceived, just at the dawn of day, that notwithstanding his exertions, the vessel had pursued them all night, and were then within a league. The rising sun convinced them to their inexpressible concern, that the vessel they perceived was a Turkish Galley, bearing on them with sails and oars.

Juſt at that inſtant, the chief mate from the forecaſtle, deſcried another veſſel under crouded ſail, which the captain rightly judged belonged to Malta; ſhe was bound to Cephalonia, and was then within about two leagues of our diſtreſſed ſhip's company. The captain gave immediate orders to brace up the yards and lay the Malteſe right on board, hoping that by their combined force, they might be able to defeat the infidels who gained on them every moment. The Turks perceived their defign, and endeavoured to prevent their junction with the Malteſe, by getting between them if poſſible, for they expected to make prize of the difabled ſhip, without any reſiſtance, which would certainly have been the caſe if they had found an opportunity of attacking her fingly; for the Chriſtians were unprovided with ammunition for an engagement with an enemy, who were not only well provided with this article, but three times their number. In this critical juncture, the commander of the Malteſe, perceiving their diſtreſs ordered a gun to be fired to leeward, which our captain anſwered by a gun, and by hoiſting Italian colours.

The Malteſe and infidels had the ſame object in purſuit, namely, that of preventing each other from getting along ſide of the diſtreſſed ſhip. A degree of maritime ſkill was diſplayed by both, on this occafion, feldom equalled and never exceeded; that of the Chriſtians, however, proved ſuperior, for juſt as the pirate was making a ſhort tack in order to run down between

them, the Maltese poured a heavy broad-side into her,
which so disconcerted the Turks that they veered the
other way, and dropt astern of the other vessel, determined to revenge their disaster on that defenceless crew
before the friendly Maltese could interfere. Mercutio
was standing by the ancient staff, when the pirates discharged a volley of small arms, a bullet penetrated his
shoulder, and his foot slipping at the same instant, he
unfortunately fell over the stern. The pirates saw him
fall, and instantly threw out a small boat called a Permagy (which they generally carry for that purpose)
and three Turks taking up the body of Mercutio, conveyed him on board the Galley. This was done so
suddenly that before the Maltese could bring their ship
to proper position for discharging another broadside,
our hero was on board the pirate, which did no other
execution than sink the Permagy and the three Turks
who had not time to get on board. This, however,
had a very good effect, for it struck a panic on the pirates, who, conceiving the Maltese to be much stronger than they really were, tacked precipitately, and
sheered off, without so much as looking after their companions, who sunk with the Permagy and were seen no
more. It was a distinguished favour of Providence that
the pirates happened to be mistaken in the opinion they
had conceived of the strength of the Maltese, for had
they charged but once more they would have discovered
their weakness, and consequently, have captured both
crews ; for they had not another round of ammunition
on board. The Maltese hoisted more sail and seemed

eager to give chace; and by this means, they were soon rid of their enemies, who employed every possible means to avoid being overtaken; consequently they were soon out of sight.

The generosity of the Maltese did not rest here. The commander ordered his boat to be hoisted out, and, attended by several young Maltese of distinction, went on board our distressed ship, where they were received with the most unfeigned gratitude. Finding Isabella drowned in tears, bewailing the fate of her beloved Mercutio, they expressed their concern for the sad event in the most pathetic manner, conjuring her, at the same time, as she valued her life, not to give way to immoderate grief; as her husband, perhaps, was alive and well, and added, that if the proper means were employed for his redemption, he might soon be set at liberty. These words seemed to inspire her with new life, she, in some measure recovered her former serenity; and, by the kind attention of the other ladies, she, at least, refrained from tears for some time.

The Maltese commander next enquired, if it was in his power to serve them in any thing further? They made him a proper acknowledgment for his kindness, and after a short consultation it was determined to convey the property of Mr. Wilcox and his fellow passengers on board the Maltese ship, the owners to accompany the Maltese to the place of their destination (Cephalonia) where they might land their property and

remain till their own veffel fhould arrive and be repaired, and in the mean time, to employ every means to
effect the liberation of their friend. The commander
of the Maltefe alfo promifed, that as foon as his fhip
was at anchor, he would procure all the affiftance poffible, and return and fee this diftrefs'd fhip fafe into the
fame port, where, he was of opinion, fhe might be
refitted as well as at Meffina ; and added, that the
Streights of Meffina (which they muft inevitably pafs
through) were extremely dangerous at that feafon of
the year.

Having unanimoufly agreed to this propofal, they
began to remove their effects, as before concerted,
which, as the utmoft diligence was employed, was
completed in a fhort time ; when taking a fhort fare-
well of their worthy captain, they went on board with
their generous deliverers, who crouding all the fail the
fhip would bear, and the wind proving favourable to
their wifhes, they caft anchor at the fouth fide of the
ifland in fiften fathom water, and a very commodious
houfe being procured, Mr. Wilcox and his friends
went on fhore, where, had Mercutio been with them,
they would have felt perfectly eafy.

'There were three Englifh fhips lying at anchor there.
The Maltefe commander went immediately on board,
and, after informing the officers of what had happened,
folicited their affiftance in behalf of the diftreffed fhip,
which was readily complied with : Three ftout long

boats were immediately fitted out with masts, sails and tow-lines; and thus equipped, proceeded to their assistance; an officer from each ship attended with their respective crews, and all under the direction of the Maltese commander, who acted the part of a pilot on the occasion.

As they used every possible exertion, they hove in sight of their object the second day about noon. They found the crew much fatigued and dispirited; however, they lost no time, but making fast their tow-lines to her head, they rowed incessantly until they brought her into the harbour, and moored her safely along side the Maltese ship, to the no small satisfaction of all parties. Having brought them all safe into port, it appears expedient to enquire into the fate of Mercutio.

The commander of the Galley in which he was carried off, was by birth, a Spaniard, who, having been guilty of some enormities in his own country, which had rendered him obnoxious, fled to Candia, where, after renouncing christianity, he obtained the command of the abovementioned Galley, and by his piracy, had accumulated a vast estate. Mercutio, when he recovered his senses, immediately enquired for Isabella, and was informed by an English slave (who had been captured some time before) that he alone had been taken in the late engagement; adding, that the Renegado was not willing to engage the Maltese, lest fortune might throw him into their hands, and therefore conceived it most adviseable to sheer off without his customary plunder.   B   Vol. II.

Mercutio's wound was examined immediately on their arrival at Candia, by a Surgeon, a native of France, and had also renounced, who very dexterously extracted the bullet, which was no easy matter, it being lodged in the upper part of the scapular, where it had lain three days and three nights. He was also very skilful and tender in applying proper dressings ; so that in a very short time he recovered the use of his hand and arm. The Surgeon, while he was dressing his shoulder one day, enquired of our hero what countryman he was, with several other questions relating to his past adventures, of which being satisfied, he told him he did not doubt but his ransom could be obtained, if he had friends in England, that would advance a sum of money for that purpose.

Mercutio answered him with reserve, but hinted that he should be glad of an opportunity of writing to his friends, if permission could be obtained. He promised to procure him the necessaries for that purpose, and would also pass his word for its being conveyed to England or elsewhere with safety and dispatch. He thanked him for his civility, and the Frenchman went immediately and brought him pen, ink and paper.

Having had an interview with the Renegado, who informed him he should have his liberty for 5000 dollars, and no less, he sat down, and wrote a pathetic letter to his father, informed him of his situation, and requesting a remittance of the sum. The letter, having first been perused by the Renegado, being dispatched, and the surgeon having pronounced him thoroughly recovered, our hero was conducted to the interior part of the island, to assist at a building, which the Renegado had undertaken to erect in the centre of a chrystal lake, about four hundred yards in diameter.

The plan was, to convey large hewn stones on a kind of raft, then to let them down gradually to the bottom so as to form a solid and level foundation, large enough for the intended superstructure. In this manner it was to be raised above the surface of the water, then a causeway to be erected from thence to the side of the lake, to convey timber and other materials to the spot. It was Mercutio's lot to be employed in the quarries, where he was obliged to labour from the dawn of day until the stars were visible at night, in company with ten other Christians, who had some time before been captured by the apostate Spaniard. Among his fellow captives, he observed one young man of an amiable countenance, who seemed to endure his sufferings with the utmost impatience and anxiety.

Our hero observed this young man's uneasiness with much concern, and would frequently reflect so attentively on the sufferings of his fellow slave, that he absolutely forgot his own—This was a happy disposition, what a pity 'tis not more general! Here all interested views were excluded, and every form set aside; they were so closely watched, and so continually kept employed, that, as yet, they had not found an opportu-

nity of difcourfing on the fubject of their woes, or of
mingling their griefs. This reflection places, in the
moft confpicuous point of view, the innate goodnefs
of Mercutio's heart. B ut to return :———

Mercutio, by frequently meditating on the vifible anxiety of this young man, began to grow remarkably pen-
five ; and he fought an opportunity of fpeaking privately to him, in order if poffible, to remove part of the
melancholy which preyed continually on his mind.

He did not wait long. One night, when all the reft,
worn down with hunger and fatigue, had forgot their
miferies in fleep, the young man, fetching a heavy
figh, uttered the following words in a low tone of voice.
" Oh my God! How long fhall I endure the pain and
ignominy to which I am at prefent condemned? Not
only deprived of my liberty, which, alone, is far dear-
er to me than life ; but cut off from all communication
with thofe I hold moft dear, which, miferable as my
fituation is, would afford me that confolation I ftand
fo much in need of now—my father has no doubt
left Italy, before the arrival of my letter, or I fhould
have heard from him before now—But what ! dare I
impioufly call in queftion, the decrees, or repine at
the difpenfations of Providence ? The immortal Jehovah has promifed that he will never forfake fuch as
repofe a confidence in his mercy; then, gracious Gód !
May I never be tempted, or being tempted, may I
never yield to the infernal fuggeftions of thofe accurfed

infidels who would have me to renounce, as they have done, the Saviour of the world, and embrace the damnable doctrine of Mahomet. No, though they should add to my present misery, the most excruciating torments that malice can devise, and cruelty execute, yet, fortified by an affiance in Thee, I shall rise superior to the persecutions of men and devils, and shall be enabled to view the bowl, the dagger and the bowstring with the utmost composure."

He paused. Mercutio had been all attention to the foregoing, and, as he lay close to his side, addressed him in the following manner. " My dear fellow prisoner, it is no small consolation to me to have met, in this miserable situation, a person of your exalted sentiments, for, though we are condemned to a state of wretched bondage, yet that God who has called us into existence, has power to deliver us out of the hands of those enemies to all good. Then let us cherish those sentiments which you have expressed, it will render our chains lighter ; our labours will become pleasant to us ; and we can eat our coarse and scanty fare, not only with content but thankfulness."

From such reflections as these, they insensibly fell into a discourse, on the different accidents by which they had been reduced to their present unhappy situation. Mercutio at the request of his companion, related (abating some particular circumstances) the whole of his adventures, from his first departure from England, to that moment. "Pray fir," faid the other, " do you remember the name of the old gentleman, who with his family failed in your company from Leghorn."

" Wilcox, fir," replied our hero. " O Heavens! my father!" exclaimed the youth, with emotion :— This declaration furprized and pleafed our hero, and alfo prompted him to afk feveral queftions concerning his adventures fince his departure from Leghorn.

" Sir," faid Wilcox, " you have been fo obliging as to give me a detail of your adventures, therefore, though my narrative is by no means interefting to any perfon but myfelf, nor the incidents of which it is compofed, furprizing or diverting, yet, to refufe a requeft fo natural, and at the fame time fo reafonable, would argue ingratitude as well as ill-breeding.

" It is now two months fince my departure from Smyrna, with a very valuable cargo, for Amfterdam ; and as wind and weather feemed to favor us, I was in great expectation of making a fhort, pleafant and profitable voyage—Heaven, however, had otherwife decreed.

" On the fifth day, at fun fet, we were attacked by the fame Rover by whom you were taken. My fhip was deeply laden, and in no condition for an engagement ;

consequently, we had no hopes of safety, except it could be accomplished by flight ; but this attempt proved abortive. After a chace of five hours the Turks overtook and grappled us. They immediately began to board us, in which they met with little or no opposition ; we being as I before observed, by no means able to prevent them, it appeared most prudent, to make a virtue of necessity, and endure patiently what we were unable to remedy.

" The Pirates after taking possession of my ship, obliged me and my crew, together with two young gentlemen from London, lately escaped from the Spaniards, to go on board the Galley. Previous, however, to our leaving, they made free to search and strip us all ; in doing which, they treated us with the utmost insult and contempt, in consequence of which several lives were lost. A Turk thrust his hand into Charles Howard's pocket, and at the same moment spit full in his face, Augustus Davenport, standing by, and observing what was done, instantly drew his sword, which they had not taken yet, and with one stroke, felled the infamous scoundrel at his feet.

" A dozen Turks instantly rushed on him, Howard and myself supported him, and a bloody battle ensued. The sailors, with the boatswain at their head, advanced to the attack, armed with handspikes, and such other weapons as they could find. The deck was soon covered with blood, and, in this stage of the battle, I received a stroke which deprived me of sense until all was over.

"When I recovered enough to take notice of the objects which surrounded me, I found my feet fast in the bilboes, and my right hand joined to the left hand of one of my sailors, by a pair of hand-cuffs. It was just clearly day when I came to myself, the most inauspicious day I ever beheld. I found myself exceeding weak and sick; indeed it was no wonder, for though I was insensible of it, I had bled incessantly, from the time I had received the wound; and the blood was scarcely stanched when I recovered my senses, as I was informed by the poor fellow to whom I was handcuffed. He said the two young gentlemen were (he believed) both mortally wounded; but they dispatched six Turks before they fell; at length, wounded, weary, and overpowered by numbers, they were mangled in a most shocking manner, and finally, hand-cuffed together as we were. The boatswain, being singled out by two of the infidels, defended himself with the utmost bravery for some time, at length they closed on him in order to throw him down; but he being both strong and active, clasped one in each arm, and by main strength, being close to the gunwale, threw himself backwards into the sea, and taking both with him, they all perished together."

"Pray, sir," said Mercutio, with impatience, "can you give me any particular account of those two young gentlemen you just now mentioned?"

"Not a very particular one," replied Wilcox, "but I understand they remain in town, under the care of a surgeon, in order to have their wounds, which, though many, are not mortal, healed; for this Spaniards is very avaricious, and notwithstanding he is much enraged at the slaughter made by them among his men, yet wishes to have them healed as soon as possible, as he, supposing them to be persons of distinction, expects a great sum for their ransom; and in this I think he is not mistaken."

"Do you suppose," resumed our hero, "there is any probability of their being sent here, when their wounds are healed?" "I am pretty well assured they will," said he; "this I am informed by a young Christian slave, whom the Renegado keeps to wait on him when on shore; and when he goes out on a cruize, leaves him to assist an old Eunuch, to whom he commits the care of all his treasure.

"This boy comes here two or three times a week, with orders to those Eunuchs who have the care of us, and are all subordinate to the old one in town. You see how difficult it is to hold any conversation even among ourselves, much more to speak to him, as he is under the strongest injunctions to hold no manner of correspondence with any of the other slaves; yet I have found means to converse with him, and find him a smart, intelligent lad, son to a very worthy man who sailed with me in the capacity of chief mate: He has

since obtained the command of a ship, and sailing last
year to the Levant, was attacked by this Renegado,
but was unable to take him or do him any damage ; his
ship being a remarkable swift sailer, escaped the Pirate ;
but this boy unfortunately falling overboard, fell into
the hands of the infidels in the same manner, only un-
wounded, as you did."

After a short pause he resumed, " My friend, I am
not without hopes that with the assistance of this lad,
the Renegado once more at sea, and Howard and Davenport here, we might find means to escape from
these devils : I am completely versed in the Arabic
language, which would greatly facilitate the enterprize. I speak this in confidence, if you conceive the
undertaking to be attended with too much hazard,
keep this a profound secret, as a discovery would be
fatal to us all.

" My dear sir," replied our hero, " you need be under
no apprehension on that score, I approve the plan, and
will freely become a sharer in the enterprize. The
two young gentlemen, you have mentioned are
intimate friends of mine ; and though I already
anticipate the pain it will give me and them on meeting each other in such a wretched situation, yet
my heart pants for the interview." The night being
far spent, and the spirits of those unfortunate youths
exhausted, they fell into broken slumbers, until
the return of day, and the appearance of their keepers arousing them to a repetition of insult and fatigue.

That day, Mirza, which is the name the Renegado had assumed when he had renounced, visited the
quarries, to take a view of his slaves, and to give some
orders to the Eunuchs who had the superintendance of
the work. He appeared, dressed in a rich Turkish habit,
and was attended by the above mentioned boy. He
inspected every part of the work minutely, and appeared very well pleased. He staid the greatest part of the
day, and when he was going away, told the chief of the
Eunuchs, he would send two more slaves the next day,
and concluded with peremptory orders to push the
work with all possible speed, and to look well to the
Christian slaves, lest they should form any cabals or
plans to escape. These orders were heard and under-
stood by Wilcox. In the course of the day, Wilcox
made several attempts to speak to the boy, but the vigilance of his keepers rendered that impracticable.

Night coming on, a cessation from labor afforded an
opportunity of resuming their nocturnal discourse,
which was the only thing that enabled them to endure
the fatigues of the day with any degree of patience.

They remained silent, until their fellow-sufferers were
asleep, when Mercutio addressed his partner in affliction :
" Well, fellow-sufferer, we have past another weari-
some day, without any prospect of relief." " Ay,"
said Wilcox, and this day has proved the most mortifying to me of any I have spent in this abominable
place : The contemptuous looks and imperious beha-

vior of that piratical villain, cut me to the very foul—
I was more than once tempted to dash his brains out
with the instrument I was laboring with. What most
mortified me, was the impossibility of speaking to the
boy; for I want to inspire him with a confidence in me,
that he may communicate all the intelligence he can
possibly collect, with regard to the motions of the Renegado, without fear."

Thus they spent good part of the time, which their
tyrannical master allotted for the recruiting of their
strength, so that they might be able to perform their
several tasks on the ensuing day : How far such rest, if
rest it may be called, would tend towards their refresh-
ment, the reader may judge, when he is informed, that
the place in which they were confined at night, was a
strong wooden building, about eighteen feet every way,
without any aperture in the sides. The roof was con-
structed of strong plank double, laid transversely, nailed
together, and perfectly flat. In the middle of the roof
was a small and strong trap-door, by which those unfortunate slaves were let in and out. A rope-ladder,
fastened to the top of the roof, served them to climb up;
then being pulled up and let down on the inside, admitted them into their apartment, the ladder being then
drawn up; the door securely locked and bolted, and
they left to their solitary contemplations. It was a
favorable circumstance, however, for those captives,
that several carpenters were at work, preparing stuff for
the inside of the new buildings ; and they were permit-

fed to gather the shavings, of which they made a common bed : On this they stretched their wearied limbs promiscuously, which was accounted a particular indulgence.

Early the next morning, the two additional slaves were conducted to the quarries, under convoy of four Turks, who belonged to the Galley. Immediately on their arrival, they were committed to the charge of the chief Eunuch, and their conductors instantly retired. Mercutio fixed his eyes attentively on the two strangers, and immediately recollected the features of his respected friends. His heart had already embraced them, but prudence forbid any other communication at that time : They did not appear to have any knowledge of him, and he found it very difficult to suppress his emotion on this occasion. That day appeared to Mercutio the longest he had ever seen : Night, however, at length put a period to the laborious employment of the day, and their guards having remanded them to their uncomfortable lodging, secured the door and left them to the most mortifying reflections.

Our hero and Wilcox had, for the convenience of discoursing together, taken their lodging in a corner as far detached from their fellow-captives as possible : To this corner they conducted the strangers.

They remained a long time silent. Mercutio, however, unable to refrain any longer, informed the strangers in a whisper, that he had been told they were from London, that he was also a native of that city, and finally requested to know their names.

The answers he received, completely satisfied him as to the identity of the persons. "You, no doubt," continued he "were acquainted with Mercutio; can you give any account of him? I was once very intimate with him, and should be happy to hear of his welfare."

"Mercutio!" exclaimed Charles; "if the person you mean, be the same with whom I once had the happiness of being acquainted, I am sorry to inform you, that he lost his life at sea in an engagement, at which I was present, and if Providence had not reserved me for more and greater misfortunes, I should have shared the same fate."

Mercutio told him, he was, happily, deceived with regard to the fate of his friend; for, he assured him, he had been in company with him in Leghorn within the last two months.

"What do you tell me?" said Charles—"Mercutio living! Pardon, me, sir, it cannot be possible—I saw him swallowed by the raging ocean, which was then of a crimson hue. No, no, I shall never see him more. Nothing short of a miracle, could have delivered him from the fury of the waves: The bare sight of the horrid conflict—the flaming ships—the maimed victims, floating on various fragments of the ships, under clouds of burning fulphur, was almoft fufficient to extinguifh life without any other accident."

" I confefs," faid Mercutio, " the prefumption in favor of your opinion is very ftrong ; but I do aver that Mercutio is ftill living, for from himfelf I had the account of his miraculous prefervation." He then began and related the whole affair, as it has already been defcribed.

" Thanks to heaven !" exclaimed Charles—" Perhaps I may yet live to fee my much loved friend—I hope he is at this moment happy : Well am I convinced, if he was acquainted with my haplefs fate, he would leave no means unaffayed, to afford me the earlieft relief."

" I am fully fenfible," replied our hero, " of the willingnefs of your friend to ferve you, was it in his power ; but that, I am forry to fay, is not the cafe, for Fortune is not yet weary of perfecuting Mercutio ; but has vigoroufly purfued him to Candia, where he is in a fimilar fituation to your own. Here, though we are refufed light, by which you might procure occular demonftration of the truth of this, yet you may reft affured, that Mercutio has, with his own mouth, informed you of his providential efcape from the dangers of the boifterous ocean, to be again captured by Mahometan Pirates."

The emotions of Augustus and Charles on this explanation, are much easier imagined than described : Each supposed the other long since dead, and consequently, all hope or expectation of meeting this side eternity, were excluded. Their discourse, for some time, was such as might reasonably be expected on so interesting an occasion, and between such sincere friends.

Charles, recounted the principal stages he had passed through since their separation.

" When the ship went down," said he, " I sunk a great way below the surface, and, indeed did not expect to rise any more, for I found myself drawn violently downwards by a power which I was not able to resist, although I used my endeavour for that purpose. At length I found my efforts, to regain the surface began to succeed, and, after being nearly suffocated, I found my head above-water, just as the Spaniards began to retreat.

" One of the Spanish ships burst into fragments just at that instant, and one of her masts, having been projected to a prodigious heighth by the explosion, fell very near me, and when it came up, I exerted all my strength to reach it, and fortunately succeeded, when I was at the point of giving up. I threw myself across the mast, fatigued and out of breath, and after recovering a little, perceived two boats tossing about among the the fragments of the ship. I called aloud for help, they heard and came to me, and took me into one of the boats, where I had not been two minutes before our own two ships returning from the chace took us on board. Though the ships were much difabled, we anchored at Portfmouth in fixteen days.

" The ships were refitted with all poffible expedition ; but the gentleman who commanded the ship in which I returned, being attacked by a bilious fever, a few days after his arrival, died before his ship was ready for fea. The admiral being informed of his death, and at the fame time of my being on board, honoured me with the command.

" The first orders I received was to convoy a fleet of tranfports, laden with troops, artillery, ammunition, fmall arms, &c. to Gibraltar ; and afterwards to cruife in the Streights three or four weeks. We failed accordingly, and meeting with fair winds and weather, made a short and profperous voyage.

" While the troops, &c. were landing, I spent great part of my time on shore with my friend Davenport, who commanded a detachment of those troops. One evening, being in company with a number of military officers, I staid pretty late, as Augustus had promifed to accompany me on board, where I conftantly flept. I fuppofe it was midnight, when we broke up, and we immediately proceeded to the place where my boat

lay. It was perfectly calm when we embarked; but
before we had got three hundred yards from shore,
the wind began to blow from the westward in a tem-
pestuous manner, and a long and heavy swell following, we were many times in danger of oversetting.
We made several attempts to reland, but in vain; the
swell drove us from the shore, and we were finally
precipitated into the Mediterranean without mast, sail,
compass, or one mouthful of food or drink. After
tossing about on the convulsed ocean two days and
nights, almost famished, and utterly divested of hope,
we espied, about the close of day, a Spanish Barca-lon-
ga, at the distance of about three leagues. It was
impossible to escape them, and indeed if that could
have been effected, we had no mind to make the expe-
riment, as death would have been inevitable: We
therefore resolved to surrender ourselves voluntarily into
their hands, and leave the event to Providence; we accordingly rowed towards them, and as they steered directly for us we soon met. They threw us a rope as soon as we
were along side, and Augustus and I went on board immediately. We were received in a very handsome
manner by the commander and officers: Our men were
taken on board, and the boat hoisted in. The commander asked me where we came from; how long we
had been at sea, and several other questions of a similar tendency. I informed him of the particulars of our
distress with which he appeared affected; then calling
an attendant ordered him to conduct us to a cabin, and

provide something to nourish us. He likewise ordered an inferior officer to see that my men were taken
care of, and that food should be given to them, but in
small quantities for a day or two.

" We did not see this worthy commander any more
that night, for the servant after having brought us
some hot wine and a small quantity of rusk, informed
us that was all he was directed to give at that time,
and that after we had refreshed ourselves, he would
show us a bed, where we might repose our weary limbs.

" We soon devoured our small repast, and though
our appetites seemed to crave a further supply we found
ourselves exceedingly refreshed ; we then went to bed,
and slept soundly till morning.

" They sailed on towards Gibraltar, their design
(as we supposed) was to reconnoitre, as they hovered
between Centra and Alberan, twenty-four hours, and
having satisfied their curiosity, took wing, and in four
days anchored in the bay of Valencia.

" The next day, we were taken on shore in my boat,
and left under guard in a house near the water-side till
further orders should arrive. We did not remain long
in this situation ; Augustus and myself were conducted to a superb building, in the east wing of the city,
where the Spanish commander, and several other officers, naval and military, were assembled,

" We were seated, and interrogated concerning our
names, country, the command each of us bore under the
crown of England; the reinforcement we had brought,
and the actual strength of the garrison.   Having passed this examination we were released with the usual
forms. All my endeavours to get my boat's crew released proved ineffectual, they were committed to close
confinement. We had each of us a good sum of money,
so that we were in no want of any thing, except liberty (we could not suppose ourselves free) and that we
intended to regain as soon as possible.

" In order to effect this, each of us purchased a
Spanish habit, and took lodgings in an obscure part
of the city where we could remain incog, till an opportunity should offer us to depart for Gibraltar, or elsewhere. Having deliberately weighed every circumstance, we concluded to travel by land to Barcelona,
and, if possible, to sail from thence to Italy.

" We soon found a vessel bound to Naples, the
passage from whence to Venice was but short; we
resolved to travel from thence to Hamburgh, from
whence it would be easy to procure passage to England. We did not suppose it safe to travel through
France.

" We set forward, and avoiding all manner of communication with travellers on the rout, arrived in
Barcelona in safety, though much fatigued.

" After a few days reſt, we made diligent inquiry
for a veſſel bound to Rome, or any other Italian port ;
we ſoon found what we wanted, and arriving at Naples, propoſed to paſs through Venice, and from thence,
as before concerted, to Hamburgh. Although this
plan appeared to be well formed, and ſeemed likely
enough to ſucceed ; yet it pleaſed God to diſappoint
our expectations ; for we had ſailed but a few leagues
from Salerno, when a moſt tremendous gale of wind
drove us notwithſtanding our moſt vigorous exertions,
on the Lipari iſles, where we ſuſtained conſiderable loſs
and damage : This, however, was but a prelude to
greater misfortunes. Our ſhip's rudder was carried
away, and every moveable on board, except our wearing apparel, a ſmall quantity of proviſion, and an
anchor of water, were thrown overboard in order to
lighten the veſſel. Unable to guide without a rudder,
and the gale continuing, we were daſhed through the
ſtreights of Meſſina with inconceivable rapidity : Deſ-
pair was depicted in every countenance, and certain
it is, that not one of the company had the moſt diſtant
expectation of ſurviving the ſtorm. A new and not
leſs terrifying proſpect ſoon preſented itſelf: The ir-
reſiſtible fury of the current ſoon diſgorged us into
the Mediterranean.

" The horror of our ſituation beggars deſcription——
To the complicated diſtreſs I have already mentioned,
diſeaſe attached itſelf ; our little proviſion being nearly
exhauſted, particularly water, the ſailors, all Italians,

fell fick, fo that it was with the utmoft difficulty we preferved the veffel from finking, two days and two nights; and I am very fure we could not have kept her above water three hours longer; but, thanks to Heaven, when we were on the point of giving all up for loft, captain Wilcox was fent to our relief.

"The moft exhalted benevolence difplayed itfelf in the treatment we received from captain Wilcox, until fortune threw us into the hands of the Pirates, which was on the third day after we forfook the wreck.

"As you have had an opportunity of converfing with the Captain, I prefume he has informed you of the particulars of our being captured, and the treatment we have received fince. We have made application to the commander at Gibraltar for relief which we are in hopes will arrive here fhortly.

"Thus I have given you a fuccinct account of our adventures, fince we parted, and do affure you, that meeting with you, though in this wretched fituation, fenfibly diminifhes the weight of my mifery, and has in a great meafure obliterated the melancholy reflections which has preyed on my mind, ever fince we had the misfortune to fall into the hands of thofe infidels."

Mercutio then briefly recited the proposals of captain Wilcox, adding, that he yet entertained hopes of regaining his liberty. They were highly pleased with it, and very readily agreed to become sharers in the enterprize.

Sleep at length arrested their eyelids, and put an end to their consultation for that time. Several days, nay weeks, elapsed but neither news nor relief arrived from Gibraltar, and but one very short interview with the boy could be procured by Wilcox. However in that, short as it was, he was convinced of the lad's integrity, who though young, was the very soul of the plan.

Fortune, at length, vouchsafed to dart her effulgent beams on them. One day as the Eunuchs were regaling themselves, after having issued to the unfortunate slaves, the scanty pittance which was appointed for their daily support, the boy arrived with a message from Mirza to the chief of them, which, when he had communicated, he hasted to the quarry, where the slaves were taking a little nourishment, if such it might be called. He informed Wilcox (a part) in a very few words, that the Renegado had, that very morning, set sail with a design of cruising off Malta, in order to intercept a Maltese ship, which he had certain information was to leave Cephalonia within two, or at the most three days, with a very valuable cargo, which he was determined to possess

himself of, or perish in the attempt. The particular
night was appointed for the execution of their plan;
the boy was to place himself at a convenient distance,
so that if the first part of the plan should succeed, he
might be in readiness to conduct them to Mirza's;
if not, that he might retreat alone, without danger of
discovery or even suspicion.

So far, then, matters were laid in a proper train,
and wore a favorable aspect.—The boy departed, un-
perceived by the Eunuchs; and our captives having
in some measure assuaged their hunger, renewed their
application to labor: The remainder of that day,
their drivers appeared to have relaxed somewhat of
their former vigilance and severity—evening approached
—hope filled their souls, and every thing seemed to
augur success.

We will leave those captives in the quarry, and
follow Mirza, who had left Candia several leagues
behind, resolutely determined to sacrifice every man
on board the ship he was in quest of, to his revenge;
which was identically the same ship's crew which
had formerly rescued that in which Mercutio left
Leghorn.

After cruising several days, Mirza was continually on the watch, perceived the Maltese heave in sight:
He was but just visible when he first espied her, consequently, he had time to make the necessary arrange-

ments. He loft no time, but inftantly gave orders to prepare for an engagement ; fwearing, at the fame time, by Mahomet that he would fend the damned Maltefe to hell, or go there himfelf, before the fetting of the fun.

The Maltefe commander, foon recollected his adverfary, and made immediate preparation for the enfuing conflict : In the mean time, the diftance between them diminifhed rapidly.

No fooner had they got within hearing, than the Renegado faluted the Maltefe, with an order to ftrike his colours ; in anfwer to which he received a well pointed broadfide, which damaged the Galley very much, both in hull and rigging, but did no other execution. This did but exafperate the Pirate the more, he again repeated his oath, of facrificing every man on board, and to that end, made a vigorous attempt to board, in order to imprefs them with terror ; but in this they were deceived ; for the Maltefe having brought fix guns to bear upon the Galley in an oblique direction, loaded with grape, difcharged them fo advantageoufly as to kill five Turks, befides Mirza, who, in a violent rage, was giving orders to grapple the fhip.

This laft difcharge put an end to the conflict, the crew on board the Galley, confifting of only five Turks and feven Chriftians, which laft were chained to the

D   VOL. II.

oar, they let her drop aftern ; the Turks finding to
their coft, they were over-matched, exerted their utmoft fpeed to efcape the Maltefe, who being deeply
laden and not in a capacity to give them chace, bore
away for Malta, and were foon out of fight and hearing
of the Pirates.

Three of the Turks remaining on board the Galley
were officers, and had followed the fortunes of Mirza
from the time of his renunciation ; and now each intended, fecretly, to feize upon the effects of their late
co-partner in guilt, as a matter of right. They were
therefore unanimous in fteering towards Candia, accordingly taking every poffible advantage of wind and
water, they arrived in their old port on that very
evening, which our heroes had appointed to make
a vigorous effort to regain their freedom.

Having moored the Galley, one of the three Turks
aforementioned, fufpecting, perhaps, his own ability
to fecure to himfelf the whole of the plunder, and
that, if his rivals fhould unite to oppofe him, they
might deprive him of any fhare, and perhaps of life,
propofed either a joint partnerfhip or an equal divi-
fion of the whole. This propofal was rejected with
contempt by the other two : Each claimed an ex-
clufive right to the difpofal of the property. Some
altercation enfuing, a rencontre took place, to which
two of the parties attacked the third, who did not
flinch a ftep, but dealt his favors fo liberally that

In two minutes he dispatched one of his antagonists, and mortally wounded the other; who in the same instant split his head to the chin, with his sabre, and both fell together.

We will turn our eyes from this horrid scene, in order to discover the movements of Mercutio and his friends. At the usual hour, the slaves were conducted to their place of confinement by their keepers, who were six in number: Their company had been that day considerably diminished, a party of nine slaves and five Eunuchs having gone to a mountain about nine miles distant, to prepare timber for sawing, and was not to return for several days. There was but one of the captives left at the quarry, who had been taken before captain Wilcox, he had been sixteen months in captivity, his name was Fitzgerald, a native of Kilkanny.

Our young adventurers, though they intended to admit all their Christian brethren, to participate with them in the success of the intended expedition, yet, they had prudently concealed their intentions from all but the boy. In the course of the last afternoon, however, they concluded it most expedient to feel the pulse of Fitzgerald, and if they found him either timid or averse to the attempt, to let it remain a secret, until the critical moment; but if, as they expected, his wishes were congenial with their own, to develope the whole plan, and hold themselves in readiness for action

They found, on examination, that Mr. Fitzgerald had long panted for such an opportunity, and when he began to perceive the drift of their conversation, the ardency of his entreaties for a full explanation of their intentions, and the avidity with which he caught every syllable they pronounced, left them no doubt of the propriety of communicating the whole business without reserve.

Fitzgerald was in raptures, and already anticipated the sweets of that liberty of which he had been so long and painfully deprived.

Having resolved on the time and mode of attack, they anxiously waited the arrival of the moment in which they were determined to free themselves from the power of the infidels or sacrifice their lives in the attempt.

It was dark when they were commanded to ascend the rope ladder; they had each concealed a short wooden truncheon between the canvas frock and the skin; Wilcox advancing to the foot of the ladder, on each side of which stood a Eunuch.

This was the critical moment! Wilcox, at one stroke, felled the one on his right, at the same instant, exclaiming, "God speed us!" which was the signal for the onset—he attacked the other; in a quarter of a minute the six Eunuchs were prostrated. The shock was fo fudden, and the ftroke, fo well directed, that refiftance was impoffible. They immediately cut the rope ladder into convenient lengths, and, taking the ftrands apart, bound them fecurely two and two together. They then raifed them up and compelled them to march to their lodging with threats of immediate death if they prefumed to utter a word; then putting them in, they locked the door fecurely, left them to their private cogitations, and departed in queft of the boy, whom they found waiting, according to appointment.

So far then their fuccefs equalled their moft fanguine expectations.—There was no time to lofe, they therefore preffed forward with all poffible fpeed, to the dwelling houfe of Mirza.

Having gained admiffion by means of the boy, they rufhed upon the old Eunuch, bound and gragged him, and locked him up in a clofet.

The boy then conducted them to an apartment, which it feems, was the grand depôt, or magazine, of thofe Pirates. Here they found all kinds of clothing, fire-arms, &c. together with a ftrong iron cheft full of money; and as every one prefent had been robbed of more or lefs by the owner of the cheft, they thought it no felony to break open and divide the contents of it among them, which they immediately did, giving the boy an equal dividend.

D 2

Having supplied themselves with arms, and money, they valued themselves on the acquisition, and began to think they were in a tolerable posture of defence.

But notwithstanding the promising state of their affairs, they remembered they were yet within the lines of the enemy, consequently in a critical and dangerous predicament; therefore wisely resolved to stay no longer there than was absolutely necessary. As they were leaving this apartment, Captain Wilcox observing a rich Turkish habit, which Mirza usually wore when on shore, took it down and folded it up, with a turban, decorated with gems of great value, saying, "Though I do make free to take these things without leave, I hope the gentleman who claims them, will excuse me, when he reflects, that he has property of mine, in his own hands to a much greater amount: At all events, I will risque his displeasure, as I expect to have particular occasion for such a habit in the course of my peregrination." Their young guide then led them into a sort of ware-house, where hung all kinds of dried provisions and fruits. Among other curiosities, he showed them a pipe of excellent Malaga, with which, notwithstanding the precepts of Mahomet and the injunctions of the Mufti, Mirza regaled himself privately. They drank a little of his prohibited beverage, and, every one taking as much of the provisions as he was able to carry, they set out for the water side where they arrived without any opposition or interruption.

Nothing could exceed their aſtoniſhment, when, at the diſtance of about three hundred yards, they perceived the identical Gally in which the Renegado had ſailed, but a ſhort time before.

This diſcovery threw them into the utmoſt conſternation. They ſtopped ſuddenly, and as their affairs ſeemed to wear a deſperate aſpect, conſulted for a few minutes on the great hazard they were expoſed to in caſe they ſhould unfortunately be diſcovered: The reſult was, to embark at all events, and if diſcovered and attacked by their enemies never to ſurrender themſelves; but conquer the infidels or periſh under the cimeter.

They embarked immediately.

The moon ſhone in its full ſplendor, and, in the moſt profound ſilence, and with all imaginable ſpeed, they began to unmoor the Galley. They perceived by the light of the moon, ſeveral perſons go on ſhore from the other Galley, and ſhape their courſe for Mirza's houſe. The boy ſaid he was certain that ſomething ſtrange had happened on board the Galley, as Mirza never remained on board after the Galley was moored; nor ſuffered his officers or ſlaves to go on ſhore, till ſhe was unloaded, and added, that he was not among them who had juſt left the Galley.

Their curioſity to know what might have happened was too powerful to be reſiſted, yet knew not how to

procure any information. Some were of opinion, that
their safety depended on putting to sea instantly, but the
greater part objected, alledging, that if in moving
from the shore, they should be observed by those on
board the other Galley, a vigorous pursuit would inevitably ensue, and as the Pirates were more in number,
and better prepared for an engagement than they, death
and destruction must be the unavoidable consequence.

The boy proposed going on board the other Galley,
and see how matters stood, observing, that as he was
perfectly acquainted with the whole crew, he could
easily invent a story to amaze them and in the mean
time, inform himself of all he wanted to know. This
proposal, however, was on the point of being rejected
for some time. It was urged that perhaps Mirza might,
notwithstanding his former custom of going on shore
immediately on his arrival, remain on board, if so,
and he should discover the boy, he would doubtless
question him, and finally extort the whole secret from
him; and that, having him in his power, he might
dispose his measures so as to defeat their whole plan
with greater facility than he possibly could, was he to
discover them just as they were leaving the shore.

All these consultations were held and the consequen-
tial resolutions taken in a very few minutes.

At length it was agreed to let the boy go, to hold
every thing in readiness to start in a moment, and, if

the boy did not return in a quarter of an hour, to put to sea and make the best of their way to some part of the main land, where peradventure they might be able to elude the vigilance of their pursuers.

The boy returned, within the time limited, bringing with him all the Christian slaves that were in Mirza's Galley. "Good news! Good news!" exclaimed the boy—"Mirza is dead—The ship he went in pursuit of, was well manned—repulsed them bravely—killed Mirza and four of his Turks: The rest brought off the Galley, glad to escape with their lives."

It is difficult to tell whether their joy or astonishment predominated: Certain it is, the message was the most welcome that had saluted their ears for a long time. They interrogated the slaves who had been released by the boy, and their story exactly corroborated with what they had already heard. These poor fellows proved to be, all but one, Captain Wilcox's sailors; they were overjoyed to find their Captain in the company: They also further informed him, that the Galley was so much damaged in the late engagement, that it would require much time and labour, before she could possibly put to sea again.

Being now assured of the death of Mirza, and of the impossibility of being pursued, if any of his adherents should attempt it, their being no craft to be had within many miles, they resolved to sail instantly. They im-

mediately caft off their moorings and committing themfelves to the protection of the Supreme Being, hoifted
fail and put to fea.   A fine breeze fpringing up, and
the veffel being a tolerable failer and in good trim, they
made a profperous and very expeditious trip to Antioch.

On their paffage, they concluded, that Captain
Wilcox, as he fpoke the Arabic language fluently,
fhould go firft on fhore in his Turkifh habit, with the
boy to attend him, and endeavour to difpofe of the
Galley. This refolution being taken, he went on fhore
early on the next morning after their arrival, and ac-
quitted himfelf fo well, that before night he difpofed of
the veffel to a merchant, for three thoufand five hundred crowns.

The next day, the merchant went on board, examined his bargain, feemed very well pleafed, and paid the
money to Captain Wilcox, who gave him poffeffion of
the Galley, rigging, &c.

They made no ftay in Antioch but proceeded immediately to Alleppo, from whence a Caravan was to
fet out in two days for Bagdat.

They remained four days in Bagdat, from whence
they proceeded to Ifpahan, where they divided the price
of the Galley, equally among the whole company.

Here they procured private lodgings, but the impatience of Captain Wilcox to see his father and other friends would not permit him to remain longer than five days in Ispahan. Mr. Fitzgerald determined to accompany the Captain as far as Ardevil on his route to Petersburgh, where he had several friends, they therefore took an affectionate farewel of Mercutio and his friends, and proceeded towards Astracan, taking the boy, by his own desire, with them.

Mercutio, Charles and Augustus began, once more, to breathe freely; and though their anxiety to return to their dearest connections and native country, was exceeding great, yet, as they had so long endured the most humiliating and painful slavery, and were now restored to new life, as it were, and liberty, they determined to spend one month in Persia, in order to recruit their wasted strength, and to make some observations on the customs and genius of the natives. In order to this, they procured each a complete Persian habit, and resolved to live as privately as possible.

They had been near three weeks in Ispahan, had visited every place of amusement, and had seen every thing worthy of the attention or observation of the curious, when they were informed that the Sophi, intended to review his cavalry on a beautiful plain at the distance of seven miles from the city.

They resolved to indulge themselves with a sight of the Persian monarch, whom yet they had not seen, and likewise the evolutions of his cavalry, whose dexterity they had frequently heard applauded.

Horses were procured, and they set out early in the day, in order to have an opportunity of choosing a convenient situation: This done, they dismounted and waited the arrival of the cavalcade.

In a short time, the approach of the Sophi was announced, by a succession of shouts, the echoes of which reverberated from the neighbouring mountains, resembled the sound of distant thunder.

Under a cloud of dust which overspread the whole plain, at length, appeared in the front of a vast body of horse, his majesty, mounted on a beautiful Arabian, and his son Abbass, presumptive heir to the Persian diadem, on his left, a youth of about fifteen.

Our hero and his friends were highly gratified with the performance of the cavalry, for though their manœuvres are quite different from those of the English horse, it must be confessed, the Persians are amazingly expert at throwing the lance, as it is no uncommon thing to see them stick a lance into a mark as small as a shilling, when on full speed, at the distance of thirty yards.

The sun shone clear, and the arms and accoutrements of the men, as well as the furniture of the horses, reflected its rays with encreased lustre.

The young prince rode a horſe young and ſkittiſh, the ſudden motion of the cavalry, in drawing their ſwords in oppoſition to the rays of the ſun, produced an inſtantaneous ſtream of light, ſimilar to a flaſh of lightning, which ſo affrighted the horſe, that he darted away with his utmoſt ſpeed, towards a ſmall, though deep and rapid ſtream called Zenderhend; the prince unable to check his career, was, in the greateſt apprehenſion of danger, borne away at an amazing rate.

It happened, fortunately, that Mercutio and his company, being well mounted, took a ſhort cut, in order if poſſible to intercept the paſſage of the affrighted beaſt, to the river. The prince called aloud for help, being then within a few perches of the ſtream when Charles and Auguſtus threw themſelves between him and it, while Mercutio undauntedly ſpurring his horſe, ſeized the prince's bridle, gently curbed and turned the foaming courſer.

The whole body was in motion, and advancing rapidly to the ſpot, where Charles and Auguſtus were aſſiſting the young prince to diſmount, who was by that time faint and almoſt breathleſs.

They had juſt placed him under a tuft of trees, when they were ſurrounded by the whole company. The Sophi diſmounted inſtantly, and, giving his horſe to an attendant, flew to his ſon, and taking his hand, affectionately enquired if he had received any hurt. Being ſa-

E

tisfied of his son's safety, he turned to Mercutio, and in the Arabic language said, " My dear friends, I " have not the happiness of an acquaintance with the " names, persons or quality of the generous preservers " of my son ; but thanks to the immortal Alla, I have " it in my power to reward their noble actions. You " will therefore accompany us to our palace, where " you shall experience a specimen of our sincere grati- " tude."

They gave their assent by the most profound obeisance. The prince being remounted, they set forward towards the city amidst the repeated acclamations of the surrounding multitude.

The beams of gratitude which darted alternately on Mercutio, Charles and Augustus, from the fine expressive eyes of Abbass, were most flattering : He would not be seperated from them ; but rode between Charles and Mercutio to the gates of the palace.

The welcome they received from Kerim Khan, the Sophi, was such as would have flattered the greatest potentates ; at the same time, it was the spontaneous production of a grateful and benevolent heart. " My " worthy friends," said he, " I have one request to " make, and that is, that while you are under our roof, " you will divest yourselves of every restraint, express " your sentiments freely, openly and candidly ; with- " out this, conversation loses all its energy, and be-

" comes languid, cold and infipid." But the uncommon attentions of young Abbafs exceeds defcription ;
the activity of his new friends; his miraculous prefervation, and his own acknowledgments, was the only
theme he wifhed to dwell on; and when his difcourfe
on this fubject was interrupted, his eyes tacitly exprefs-
ed the ardour of his feelings.

The Sophi, at firft fuppofed them Perfians ; but,
perceiving his error, he defired to be informed of their
names, country, and profeffions, whether naval, military or commercial. Mercutio then briefly related
their adventures, as they have been in the foregoing
pages.

Kerim liftened to the tale with aftonifhment ; regretted their loffes ; fympathized in their misfortunes,
and rejoiced in their efcape. He exprefled, in the
moft animated terms, his fatisfaction in the difcovery of
their being natives of England. " I have long had the
" moft ardent defire to cultivate an acquaintance with
" his Brittanic majefty. I am convinced that a com-
" mercial correfpondence might be carried on very ad-
" vantageoufly by the way of Ruffia ; but the Em-
" prefs is jealous of the power of your countrymen,
" and is afraid if they once get footing on the Cafpian
" fhore, the navigation of that fea will be monopolized
" by them ; and her commercial interefts in this part of
" the world totally extinguifhed. Was this not the cafe,
" I fhould be happy to open a communication with

" England which I am fatisfied would be to our mutual
" advantage ; however, it is not impoffible that thefe
" matters may be brought about in the courfe of a few
" years.

He then afked feveral queftions concerning the conftitution, laws, &c. of England ; the anfwers to which,
made by Mercutio, were fo perfpicuous and fatisfactory,
that Abbafs, as well as his father, was both delighted
and furprifed.

They were fummoned to dinner, which confifted of
the moft choice viands, fweet-meats, milk, rice, &c.
after which they retired to the magnificent gardens of
the palace, which are varioufly and beautifully difpofed, as well as very extenfive.

Here the Sophi gave a loofe to unreftrained converfation, in the courfe of which, he requefted them to
give him a defcription of the ftanding forces of Great-
Britain, naval and military, together with the general
character of the natives.

In compliance with this requeft, Charles gave him a
very particular defcription of the naval eftablifhment ;
the mode of difcipline at fea and in action ; the number
of fhips then in actual fervice together with the number
of guns, weight of metal, and number of men in each.

The military laws, cuſtoms and manœuvres were next copiouſly treated of by Auguſtus, who, by a diligent application, had acquired the moſt perfect knowledge of tactics.

Kerim expreſſed the utmoſt aſtoniſhment at the power of Great-Britain: He was perfectly amazed, that ſo ſmall a nation ſhould ſupport ſuch a formidable naval force, when the whole Perſian empire could not afford twelve ſhips.

Night approaching, Mercutio intimated to his friends, that it was time for them to withdraw, the Sophi oppoſed this warmly. "If, (ſaid he) it is convenient and agreeable to you, to make this your place of reſidence during your ſtay in Iſpahan, it will afford me a ſuperior degree of ſatisfaction : I have experienced more real pleaſure in your company this day, than I ever had before. I beg you will not refuſe me ; there are a number of ſubjects on which I wiſh to diſcourſe with you ; many things of which I would gladly be informed, and if I miſs this opportunity, it is more than probable, I may never meet ſuch another.

They bowed conſent, and thanked him for the honour he intended them.

The Sophi conducted them to a grand ſaloon, illuminated with waxen tapers, they were ſeated on the floor which was covered with carpets of the firſt mage

nificence. A grand collation being served up, they regaled themfelves fumptuoufly ; in the mean time, they
were highly entertained by a concert of vocal and in-
ftrumental mufic, performed entirely by females, from
whom they were feperated by a curtain of green filk
only.

This unexpected entertainment, afforded our European friends the higheft fatisfaction, which they figni-
fied to the Sophi, who obligingly anfwered, " I wifh
it was in my power to make every moment of your
ftay in Perfia yield you frefh delight ! But come,"
added he, addreffing Mercutio, " it is yet early, you
have not forgotten my requeft, I am impatient to be
part cularly informed of the general character of your
countrymen, their manners and cuftoms in private life."
Our hero complied, and fo animated was his defcription, and fo pertinent his remarks, that the Sophi was
delighted almoft to enthufiafm : He declared, that if
they would confent to remain in Perfia, he would promote them to pofts of the fecond dignity in the Empire. To this they made no anfwer, but by an inclination of the head. The proper time for retirement
being come, thefe youths, who, but a few days paft,
where conducted to a bed of fhavings, and locked up
in a den, dark and noifome, were now conducted in
a refpectful manner, to one of the moft fuperb apartments in a palace.

Let no man defpond ; for there is no cafe fo defperate, on this fide eternity, but a parrallel may readily
be found ; but fuppofing one in which this might be
found impoffible, ftill, defpondency is unavailing, impious to the laft degree, unjuftifiable, and unmanly :
Many have precipitated themfelves into the jaws of
death, when five minutes reflection would have prevented the rafh deed : In the very point of time, perhaps when their affairs had taken the moft profperous
direction. That power in whofe hands are the iffues of
life and death, will not permit a rational being, who
confidentially depends on his affiftance, to fink under
his miferies, however great or numerous : Mercutio in
the greateft of his troubles (and they were not trifling)
never quitted the grafp he had taken on hope.

The next day they were prefent at a grand levee of
the Perfian nobility ; among thefe, were three governors
of provinces, with grand retinues : They here difcovered that fycophantic adulation, and abject fawning
was not confined to the Englifh court ; much of this
kind of artillery was difcharged, by thefe turban'd de-
pendents, not only at the Sophi but at the heir apparent.

This difgufting parade concluded, and the crowd
withdrawn, the Sophi with his fon and felect friends
retired to the faloon to dine.

After dinner, " you fee my friends," faid the monarch, " the pomp and flavery of a prince. It is my
wifh and intention to render my fubjects, of every defcription, as happy as their fituations and circumftances
will poffibly admit ; I am particularly careful in my
choice of governors, and officers of every department ;
I endeavour by mildnefs and benevolence to fhow them
the line of conduct I would have them purfue towards
the lower orders of my people, and though I endeavour
by all means to infpire thofe about me with franknefs
and fincerity ; yet I always perceive in their behaviour
and converfation a conftrained imitation of fincerity
only ; their fpeeches are all ftudied, are all calculated
to flatter the ear, and miflead the judgment : They do
not fpeak the language of the heart : I perceive and
defpife their meannefs ; yet I am condemned to liften
to adulation, which my fenfe can never approve. One
principal reafon of my anxiety to retain you in Perfia is
this, I would fain fpend my vacant hours in the company of a few felect friends, who would unfold the real fentiments of their hearts, on all occafions, without referve. With fuch friends, I fhould enjoy all that
fatisfaction of which my fubjects fuppofe me fully poffeffed. Frequent converfe with perfons of this defcription would afford a moft comfortable relaxation to my
mind ; would give a relifh to thofe avocations which
now appear tedious to me : I fhould then be indeed
as cheerful as I fometimes only appear to be,

" My son Abbafs is very defirous to acquire a knowledge of the Englifh language, and confiders it as no
very difficult tafk, if you, faid he to Mercutio, would
undertake to be his preceptor for fome time, which,
as you fpeak the Arabic fluently, would to you be no
difagreeable employment; for I am fure he efteems you
very highly, and will follow your directions implicitly.

" The European mode of military difcipline I have
often heard of, but ever fince I heard its principles fo
clearly explained by you, have had a defire to introduce it in my army; now you, (turning to Auguftus,)
being fo completely verfed in the whole art, together
with its fundamental principles, are the only perfon
who could affift me in carrying this into execution.

" If I could prevail on you to remain with me fome
time longer, fuppofe two months, I think in that time,
my plan will be in a ftate of tolerable forwardnefs, and
the time fo fpent will conduce more to my happinefs
than any period of my paft life."

After the moft folicitous enquiry for each others
fentiments, by the paffage of the eye, Mercutio, having made the neceffary difcovery, replied, " Beft of
princes, it is a long time fince I parted with my deareft friends and relatives, the greater part of which
time I have been perfecuted by fortune—driven by
reiterated difafters into every quarter of the globe; and
am ftill liable to fall into the hands of fome of the pow-

ers actually at war with Great-Britain; to avoid which was our principal defign in paffing through the Ruffian territories, which muft greatly retard us in our return, as well as prolong the time of our abfence from thofe whom we love and venerate. The ardency of our wifhes to return to our native foil, to embrace thofe dear relatives, your majefty will readily agree, muft be extreme; notwithftanding the cogency of thofe reafons for our moft prompt exertions to acclerate our return to England, I perceive, by the countenances of my friends, and my own feelings, that you have gained your point." Charles and Auguftus confirmed his judgment. Nothing could have exceeded the fatisfaction of the Sophi on this occafion. " My dear friends," faid he, " my heart diftended with gratitude, for paft favors, now overflows. To offer, or even to conceive a return equal to your unmerited generofity, infinitely exceeds my power: My utmoft endeavours, however, fhall not be wanting, and my inability, I truft, will meet an excufe. Abbafs fhall be your friend: He loves you already with the fondnefs of a brother; and if the Perfian Empire contains any thing worthy of your acceptance, only point it out, and I will fhow you how much Kerim efteems you, by the freedom of the grant; and the pleafure he will take in having it in his power to difcharge a part of the obligations your kindnefs has laid him under." Our hero affured the Sophi, that they confidered the honors he had conferred on him and his friends, much more than adequate to any fervices they had or could render him.

Some difpatches arriving, interrupted their mutual acknowledgments.

Thus our young friends whofe affairs, but a very
fhort time paft, were moft defperate, and prefented
not even the moft faint and diftant profpect of alteration
or amendment, were in an exalted degree of favour,
and clofeft habits of friendſhip with a great and amiable prince; and held in the higheft degree of efteem by
all his nobles. Thus it is that Providence heaps, by
fudden and almoft imperceptible tranfitions, unfore-
feen, unexpected, and undeferved bleffings on mankind, even when every ray of hope is extinguifhed, and
after the fell ufurper, defpair, has eftablifhed an abfo-
lute fway over the empire of the foul. This reflection
conveys an inftructive admonition to fuch as are, either by conftitution or habit, moft liable to flinch from
the ftroke of adverfity, and to bend under the weight
of misfortunes which are unavoidable, and which are,
more or lefs, fooner or later, in one fhape or another,
the inevitable entail of the human family, to place an
unbounded affiance in that Omnipotent Being, whofe
Almighty will directs and governs the great and im-
mutable fprings of life and motion; for as no fituation,
however obfcure, is capable of fecluding us from obfervation; no caution on our part, however nice, can
evade his penetration, not even for a moment; nor a
poffibility of any fcheme of Providence being counter-
acted, or rendered abortive by the moft fuitable con-
trivances of man; therefore, our interest as well as

duty is to repose an unlimited confidence in him, who never withholds his interposition and favour, on every proper occasion. Despondency argues a degenerate mind. He who doubts, tacitly arraigns the justice and mercy, or wisdom and power of God. But to return:

Our hero entered on his new occupation the very next day, as also did Charles and Augustus. As Charles had but an imperfect knowledge of the military discipline, it was necessary he should become the first of Augustus's pupils, in order to attain such a proficiency as would qualify him to assist his friend. Accordingly, in a very few days they were ready for business. They then formed a small corps, composed of the commanding officers of the several regiments, which, by the Sultan's devise, were to be immediately disciplined. This being accomplished, similar squads were formed of the subalterns, who took so much delight in the manoeuvres, and so highly esteemed their teachers, that in a very short space they were fully capable of forming their respective companies, which was immediately undertaken.

The Sophi constantly attended at the performance of their exercises, and expressed his approbation in terms, which at the same time that they indicated the highest satisfaction, afforded the most complete gratification to both tutors and pupils, and encouraged them to prosecute their labours with unremitting diligence and delight: The officers were no less diligent than the So-

phi, which was a fource of pleafure to Charles and
Auguftus.

If Kerim was elated at the vaft progrefs of his officers in the European exercife, the fuperior fatisfaction
he enjoyed in the proficiency of his fon, in pronouncing
Englifh, which by this time he did with a degree of cor-
rectnefs really aftonifhing, may readily be conceived.
The Sophi requefted his European friends to difcourfe
with Abbafs in no other language thenceforward.

The Perfian commanders having new modelled their
feveral regiments, four hours each day was fpent in
manœuvring the troops, for near two months ; this
being always performed under the immediate eye of
the Sophi, and the moft fcrupulous fuperintendance of
Charles and Auguftus ; they went through the various
evolutions with all the exactnefs and dexterity of ve-
terans. In the mean time, Mercutio and his pupil
were not idle : Abbafs pronounced Englifh with an
uncommon degree of accuracy, and expreffed the moft
ardent defire to be farther inftructed : Even fo far as to
read and write it. The Sophi being exceedingly anxious to have the mind of his fon ftocked with every fpecies of ufeful knowledge, fent to Cafbin, to an Englifh merchant who dwelt there, requefting him to fend
all the Englifh books he could poffibly fpare. He fent
feveral, and promifed to write to a correfpondent in
Peterfburgh, to procure him a collection from London,
by which means he would be able to furnifh his majefty
with what books he wanted.

Mercutio would have been as happy as he had ever been since his departute from England, but reflections on the uncertain fate of Isabella frequently embittered those sweets, which the conversation of his friends and the favour of the Sophi afforded; yet hope, all reviving hope, would come to his aid, would present to the eye of his fond imagination, the strongest probabilities of her being restored to his possession: They were separated, but she was left in the company of friends, who would treat her with tenderness and affection, until his return to England.   These thoughts re-animated him, and again he became cheerful.

His pupil was of a sweet disposition, and he viewed him in a two fold light, as a tutor highly esteemed, and as a brother beloved.   The Sophi was continually heaping honours on him and his friends, and recommending them to the attention of his noble son, who indeed manifested the most unfeigned regard for them. The Sophi declared, that he considered the frequent intervals in which he was indispensibly separated from them, as so many interruptions to his happiness.

We will now take leave of them and enquire into the fate of old Mr. Wilcox and his company.   The reader will readily recollect that we left them at Cephalonia, full of grateful acknowledgements to the Maltese commander, who had so generously rescued them from the hands of the Pirates.

As it required fome confiderable time to refit the veffel, Mr. Wilcox rented a houfe ready furnifhed, for the accommodation of his whole company. The moment the afflicting news of Mercutio's difafter was communicated to Ifabella, fhe fhriek'd aloud, and fell into the arms of Terentia infenfible, in which fituation fhe remained fo long, that almoft every hope of her recovery was extinguifhed. At length, however, with a long and heavy figh, fhe once more opened her eyes to the light. After fixing her eyes fteadfaftly on the company around her, with anxious folicitude for a few moments, and miffing her beloved Mercutio, fhe exclaimed, "Gracious heavens! is he then gone? And are we for ever feparated? Oh no! Death has parted us for a fhort fpace, but will foon reunite our fpirits forever!" Her fpirits being exhaufted, fhe dropt from her feat motionlefs, and, in that fituation remained near three hours; however, by the affectionate affiduity of her friends, aided by medical applications, fhe recovered her fenfes: Still fhe remained feeble and languid; a fettled melancholy diffufed itfelf over her countenance, fhe appeared totally indifferent, and, at certain intervals, infenfible of what was faid or done in her prefence.

The fhip repaired, and all matters fettled, they once more fet fail for Amfterdam. The irrefiftible current fetting out of the Streights of Meffina, with a fharp North Weftern breeze, bore them over to the weftern extremity of the ifland of Candia: They were within

about two leagues of Cape St. John, when they difcovered a fail ftanding out of Serigo, with an apparent
defign of boarding. Our unfortunate voyagers, now
perceived to their inexpreffible grief and confternation,
that it was a Turkifh Pirate ; and before they had time
to adopt any means of efcape or defence, they were
grappled and boarded by the infidels. The captors
conveyed their prize to Gallipoli, where they difpofed
of the fhip, and taking their captives on board the galley, penetrated the Marmora to Conftantinople.

They were conducted through the ftreets in the habits
of flaves, (the Turks having ftripped them of every thing
valuable) fhackled like criminals, to a houfe appointed
for their reception, until the Pirate fhould otherwife
difpofe of them. He left them under the care of three
Turks, with orders to provide fufficient provifion for
their fuftenance ; and to keep them fecurely till his return.

He came back in the evening, leading in two beautiful women in rich Perfian habits : After feating them
on the carpet, he beckoned to Ifabella, who followed
him with her eyes fixed on the ground, without uttering a fyllable. They were met at the door, by a tall
man in the habit of a Perfian nobleman, to whom Ifabella
was furrendered, and the Perfian delivered to the Renegado a purfe, with which he inftantly difappeared.

The Perfian began to difcourfe to her in a language which fhe neither underftood or attended to : Equally regardlefs of him and his difcourfe, fhe walked penfively after him to the bank of the Bofphorus. He waved his turban, and in a few minutes a boat came from a veffel which lay at a fhort diftance.

However indifferent the forlorn Ifabella had hitherto been with regard to what happened, or whither fhe was going, it was a difficult tafk to get her into the boat : She fcreamed aloud for Eugenio, Terentia, and the reft of her unhappy fellow-captives. Her fenfibility being awakened, fhe exclaimed in the moft piteous accents : " Why, oh! why am I fingled out a victim to the dif-pleafure of heaven ? Oh death! execute inftantly; thy irrevocable commiffion, and extinguifh my miferies and exiftence with one ftroke !"

The Perfian, taking advantage of her diforder, feized that opportunity of taking her on board the boat, while fhe rent the air with her lamentations. They were quickly conveyed to Trebifond, a port in the black fea, where they difembarked, and purfued the neareft route to Ifpahan, the place of the Perfian's refidence.

Unpropitious and defperate as her circumftances actually appeared, had any friendly voice whifpered in the ear of Ifabella, only a bare probability of Mercutio's being in Ifpahan, how would her tender bofom have glowed with delight! How pleafing her dreams! How

tranquil her flumbers! But alas! the haplefs fair one
muft fubmit to clofe confinement; to the bafe, humiliating, fulfome propofals of an infamous fcoundrel;
deftitute of every fupport, under fuch complicated ca-
lamity, but a confcioufnefs of her own inflexible fidelity and virtue—Or had Mercutio entertained the
moft diftant idea of her actual fituation, how would his
bofom have been convulfed with contending paffions!
With what eager hafte would he have communicated
the diftracting, yet pleafing tidings, to his friends, and
having engaged their affiftance, would he not have
exerted fpeed, almoft impoffible, until he had regain-
ed his treafure; refcued her from the impious hands of
her intended ravifher, or nobly perifhed in the laudable
attempt?—This indulgence, however, was withheld.

We will now turn to our hero and his companions,
who had engroffed all the efteem and confidence of the
Sovereign of Perfia; were frequently and attentively
confulted on political matters, and were univerfally
careffed by the Perfian nobility.

Our three friends returning from an excurfion with
fome of the principal officers of the Sophi's houfhold,
and paffing through an avenue not far diftant from the
palace, were alarmed with repeated fhrieks of a woman in apparent diftrefs. They drew up as near to a
window of the houfe whence the cries proceeded, as
they conveniently could; and though they were not
able to diftinguifh the particulars, they heard enough

to convince them that some great injury was about to be offered to the person, whose cries had alarmed them, which, it was their duty to prevent if possible. They instantly knocked at the door, and demanded immediate entrance. After repeated applications, they were commanded to begone; this command was accompanied with threats, in case of refusal. The cries were now redoubled, which prompted them to unite their strength, and force open the outer door: This was performed instantaneously, and when they had almost reached the scene of action, they were suddenly intercepted by the master of the house. He placed his back to the chamber door, and demanded their business, at such an unseasonable hour; then, without waiting for a reply, brandishing a poniard, commanded them to depart immediately.

His menaces, however, were thrown away: They insisted on seeing the person whose shrieks and cries had drawn them thither. At that very instant the chamber door flew open, and a lady appeared with her garments much discomposed, her hair dishevelled and eyes suffused in tears. She earnestly requested them to rescue her from destruction; and added, her life was on the point of being sacrificed, for daring to attempt the preservation of her body from pollution, which this vile wretch, said she (pointing to the Persian) was determined on accomplishing if possible. "Your timely interposition, will, I trust," continued she, " be the means of preserving my life, and what is far more dear to me, my honour." Tears stifled her further utterance.

Mercutio advanced, in order to take her hand, when the Perfian aimed a ftroke at his breaft with his poniard ; but our hero, parrying received it in his left arm.

Charles and Auguftus inftantly feized the Perfian, threw him, and wrefted the poinard from his hand : The lady fprang into the arms of Auguftus, and moft pathetically craved his protection. He affured her of the moft ample protection and refpectful treatment, until redrefs could be obtained.

Mercutio and Charles had, in the mean time forced the old Perfian into the chamber, and locked the door ; they then left him, raving like a frantic bedlamite, and bore off their prize, exulting in the fuccefs of their adventure, and fully refolved to fee ample juftice adminiftered to the afflicted fair one, who accompanied them in filence, except fobs which involuntarily burft forth from her confufed bofom.

Auguftus committed the lady to the care of the keeper of the Harem, for that night, with orders that fhe might not be interrupted by any perfon, until he faw her again : The night being far advanced, our hero and his friends retired to reft, intreating the lady to compofe herfelf, affuring her fhe was in honorable hands, and that they would fee her juftified in the morning.

The lady, being conducted to a proper apartment, threw herfelf on a fopha, where fhe lay till morning, revolving in her mind the various circumstances of the preceding evening. The treatment she had already experienced from her deliverers, indicated the height of benevolence and honour; but who, or what manner of men they were, or what could stimulate them to expose themselves to such manifest hazard, in defence of a total stranger, appeared to her an inexplicable riddle: The result of those reflections, at the end of a sleepless night, was a resolution to hold herself prepared for the last distress, and never to survive the loss of honor.

In the morning, our adventurers obtained an early audience, when they informed the Sophi of every part of their evening's adventure, and finally requested him to have the parties face to face.

Kerim accordingly commanded an officer, accompanied by Augustus, to go and bring the offender into his presence forthwith. In the mean time, the chief Eunuch was sent for the lady: He soon returned leading her by the hand. Her eyes were steadfastly fixed on the floor; and her mind was so deeply engaged in ruminating on her untoward situation, that she took no manner of notice of the Sophi or of any other person present.

The monarch surveyed her with the most acute attention for some minutes, and, judging by her habit that she must be a native of Turkey, he addressed her in the Arabic language:

" Young woman," said he, " we have been informed of the particulars of your case, and are determined to render you impartial justice.   Do not suffer fear to oppress, nor grief to disconcert you, you are in the presence of those who will not permit either subject or foreigner to be abused, or insulted with impunity, within the limits of the Persian dominions ; but will administer justice to all with an equal hand.

The lady perceived by his discourse that she was in the presence of a monarch, and also a rational being, whose mind appeared fraught with sentiments of humanity and virtue ; she was therefore, encouraged to prostrate herself before him, and to implore his protection, which she did in terms so pathetic, as constrained him to rise from his seat, raise her up in the gentlest manner, and assure her, her request should be granted.

He desired her to be composed, and was conducting her to a seat beside his own, when a scence was exhibited which arrested the attention of the whole groupe, and filled them with astonishment !

Mercutio, whose eyes had been rivetted upon her, from the moment she entered, springing from his seat, caught her in his arms, and eagerly exclaimed " Immortal Jehovah ! My long lost Isabella !—Rejoice with me, my friends !—Behold the dear partner of my soul !"—She fainted—The Sophi was almost petrified with astonishment—Charles sprang to her assistance—She revived, and in falt'ring accents pronounced: " What means this univerfal trepidation which has feized my frame?—It cannot be—'Tis all illufion—No, no, my dear, my beloved Mercutio is no more—cruel fate has feparated us for ever—No more fhall I gaze, with delight unutterable, on his"——Tears arrefted the organs of fpeech—fhe could no more.

" Be compofed my deareft life, faid Mercutio—You are not deceived my love,—Mercutio once more clafps his deareft Ifabella in his enraptured embrace. Arife my love, here are none but the moft gracious, beft of friends."

A glow of the higheft fatisfaction was depicted on every brow; joy fparkled in every eye, and a kind of tumultuous pleafure expanded every bofom prefent.

The Sophi was the firft to congratulate our hero on this happy turn of fortune; and Abbafs juft now accidentally entering, joined in the general joy, and completed the happy groupe.

Auguftus now entering, informed his majefty that the prifoner was without, and, at the fame time, delivered to them a poniard of great value, which he had forced from the prifoner in the very moment he had raifed it with an intention to give him a mortal ftab.

Charles, in a few words, difclofed to Auguftus, the particulars of the difcovery which had been made in his abfence ; he heartily congratulated his friend on his happinefs, and wifhed him a long continuation of it.

" Bring the culprit before us," faid Kerim.

He was immediately introduced, and proved to be a perfon who, by the art of diffimulation, had ingratiated himfelf with his prince fo, that he had conferred fome of the greateft dignities in the Empire on him, and, until this period, confidered him as one of his moft faithful fubjects : Thus, as in many other inftances, was a humane and benevolent fovereign made dupe to the artifice of a defigning, treacherous villain.

It appeared in the courfe of his examination, that he had deluded the two females, whom he had exchanged for Ifabella from the Harem of the Sophi, under the fpecious pretence of conveying them out of the Perfian dominions, and of providing them the means of returning to their friends and country ; his real intention being to detain them privately in his own houfe ; to make them fubfervient to his defires, and then to difpofe of them to the greateft advantage. The poniard which was prefented to the Sophi by his brother, he had alfo ftolen out of the palace about three months before the time we are fpeaking of. He, knowing the inflexibility of his prince againft fuch atrocious offenders, and confcious guilt overwhelming him with defpair, confeffed, that if he had fucceeded in his defign on Ifabella, his intention was to have difpofed of her in the fame manner in which he had the other two, after keeping her as long as he should judge convenient.

"Ungrateful caitiff!" exclaimed the Sophi, with fire darting from his eyes, "I should as readily have suspected my own son of abusing my confidence as thee, on whom I have heaped favors without number or measure: The finger of justice has at length pointed out the baseness of thy contaminated heart, and the sword which shall punish thee for thy crimes is already unsheathed. Thou hast, (continued he,) forfeited every claim to mercy by thy treachery; but thy ingratitude merits immediate and excruciating torture:" These words were pronounced in such an ireful and emphatic tone of voice and gesture, that the wretched criminal appeared to be more dead than alive, "Take him away," said Kerim; " to-morrow by the rising of the sun let the keen cimeter sever the traitor's head from his vile body—Let his houses be razed to the ground, his enclosures burnt to ashes, and every thing that heretofore bore his name, be totally annihilated, and swept from the face of the earth, so that no vestage of such a vile miscreant may remain, to pollute my good subjects."

While this business was transacting, Mercutio conducted Isabella to another apartment, where they spent a considerable time in the most affectionate enquiries and congratulations; in the renewal of their former protestations of eternal love and fidelity; those endear-

G   VOL. II.

ing expreſſions to which they had ſo long been ſtrangers, were now heighten'd into rapture, by the pleaſing reflection of their miraculous eſcape, from thoſe dangers, apparently inſurmountable, which threatened their eternal ſeparation. They humbly and fervently admired the wonderful, nay, incomprehenſible means employed by the Almighty, in the preſervation of unworthy mortals, and returned mutual and ſincere thanks, for the much deſired, ſuperior bleſſing, of being once more reſtored to each other: The ſituation they were then placed in, leaving but one wiſh, and that was to be in England.

They were ſummoned to breakfaſt, during which the Sophi was laviſh of his encomiums on the accompliſhments of Iſabella, declaring as his opinion, that ſhe ſurpaſſed all the ladies he had ever beheld, in a ſuperlative degree.

The crimſon glow which overſpread the lovely countenance of Iſabella, joined to the ſweet embarraſſment which eclipſed that penſiveneſs, under which ſhe laboured at her firſt appearance before the Sophi, ſeemed to confer graces too exquiſite to be poſſeſſed by a mortal.

Breakfaſt paſſed, our friends jointly and earneſtly ſolicited the Sophi for a mitigation of the puniſhment of the unhappy victim of his diſpleaſure, on whom he had paſſed ſentence of death.

" My invaluable, beſt friends, I am under ſo many and great obligations to each, and all of you, that I conſider it as a duty incumbent on me, to grant you any and every requeſt, conſiſtent with reaſon, and the regard I have for you, and that is not derogatory to my own dignity and the good of my ſubjects. On the other hand, give me leave to aſſure you, that my inclinations are in exact co-incidence with this duty ; and as I abhor every ſpecies of ingratitude in others, ſo I would not be even ſuſpected of it myſelf.

" With regard to your preſent requeſt, it ſhall be granted—But do not ſuppoſe that I will grant him an entire remiſſion."

" All we requeſt, is that his life may be ſpared ; we conceive any greater extent of indulgence might be productive of evil conſequences, by affording encouragement to others, to perpetrate ſimilar crimes, under an expectation of ſhelter (beneath your majeſty's royal clemency) from the juſt vengeance of the laws of their injured country."

" In Mount Taurus are wilds impervious for all but wild beaſts of the foreſt, and thoſe criminals whoſe multiplied enormities have procured them a habitation among them : Thither I will baniſh him, to ſubſiſt on what he can procure by the gun and ax ; both which, together with a quantity of ammunition he will be ſupplied with by the officer appointed for that purpoſe,

and if he is found within the cultivated part of our dominions within the space of twenty years, certain and
immediate death shall be the consequence."

Orders were instantly given to convey the prisoner to
his place of exile, under a strong guard. When he
was informed of the change of his sentence, he stamped, cursed and swore like a raving bedlamite—He cursed the Sophi's mistaken lenity, and swore he would
rather die a thousand deaths than be carried into ignominious slavery, and finally threatened to lay violent
hands on his keeper, who turning short, made a stroke
at him, which deprived him of his right ear : He then
ordered his hands to be bound fast behind him, and, a
proper guard being appointed, he was sent off on his
way to Taurus.

We perceive in the fate of this man a striking instance
of the invariable justice of Providence, in the punishment of offenders of this description. Had this unhappy, ungrateful wretch ; taken but half the pains, to be
what he pretended to be, as he did to appear to be what
he was not, he might have terminated his days high in
the favor and confidence of his prince, and what is of
far more estimation, in a consciousness of having performed his duty in a becoming manner : His last sun,
instead of being enveloped in remorse and despair,
would have set serenely, and his soul would have taken
her flight, on the wings of tranquillity, to realms of
bliss.

'Two months having elapsed after the restoration of Isabella, Abbass having attained so great a proficiency under our hero's tuition, as to be able to express himself, on any subject, in a very good style of English; he also read and wrote it with a degree of judgment and accuracy, far exceeding every expectation which could have been rationally formed; the select troops completely versed in the use of the musquet and bayonet, and the desire of returning to Europe, pervading the minds of our hero and his friends, they conceived it high time to communicate their wishes to the Sophi, and obtain his leave to depart.

'They embraced the earliest opportunity of breaking the matter to Kerim. Mercutio undertook this task, and was seconded by Charles and Augustus. It was not without manifest symptoms of regret, that this amiable monarch gave his assent to the separation. " Heaven knows," said he, " with what reluctance I shall pronounce the last adieu, to persons who have, so extensively contributed to the emolument of my family, my Empire, and to my own private happiness.— When you forsake me, every moment of relaxation from public business will be employed in the contemplation of the many pleasing hours spent in your company and conversation. If riches or honours had charms sufficient to attract your attention—to retain you in Persia, how willingly! How eagerly would I confer them! But alas! as that cannot be; since you so ardently desire to return to your native country and

connexions, which, I muſt confeſs, is both natural
and laudible, be it our care to ſee you properly accommodated ; to ſee you reſpectfully treated until your
departure, and then ſafely conveyed to the frontiers of
Perſia.   Let me have notice ten days, at leaſt, before
you ſet out ; and in the mean time, let me enjoy as
much of your company as poſſible, conſiſtent with
your own convenience.

Buſineſs of moment demands my attention : Abbaſs, ſtay with our friends——Embrace every opportunity of improving yourſelf by their precepts and ex-
amples—Loſe not a moment ; but be not burthen-
ſome." He retired, leaving them full of ſilent approbation and exalted eſteem.

The young prince was no leſs affected with the news
of their intended departure, than was his royal Sire.
He lamented the privation of their ſociety, as if it had
already taken place, in terms at once expreſſive of his
ſincere gratitude and affectionate eſteem.   He expreſſed
a deſire to accompany them to England, and moſt ardently requeſted Mercutio to exert his influence with
his father, in order to procure his approbation to the
meaſure. He conceived it no difficult matter, and reiterated his requeſt with ſo much earneſtneſs, that our
hero promiſed to preſs the matter home at the next interview.

They were sitting, one fine evening, on the top of the royal palace, and while they enhaled the gentle zephyrs, anticipated the pleasure of embracing their friends in England in a short period ; having agreed to give the Sophi the notice he required, the ensuing morning.

Abbafs appeared, and with an embarraffed air, informed them that his royal father, had just received fome important difpatches; and requefted their company, if they were difengaged.

They immediately waited on his majefty, and found him in earneft difcourfe with his firft minifter, or vizier. He arofe, faluted them with his ufual cheerfulnefs, and caufed them to be feated. " My moft ineftimable friends," faid he, " I am affured you are at a lofs to divine the meaning of this fudden convention ; I will, therefore, in a few words, remove your fufpenfe by informing you that four of our diftant provinces, namely, Chorazan, Adirbeitzan, Kilan and Sableftan, are in a ftate of actual rebellion. I have certain information of this by a private letter from a faithful fubject in Herat. He informs me that the governor of Chorazan, (a Ruffian) in order to effect a revolution in the Empire, has diffeminated the feeds of fedition far and wide, by encouraging a fpirit of licentioufnefs among the lower ranks ; and by bribes, and promifes of great rewards in territory, and pofts of honor and profit, among the better fort ; he has poifoned the minds of the greater part of the inhabitants of those provinces. My friend writes further, that he has garrisoned Asterabat, a convenient port on the Caspian sea, in order to keep open a communication with his country-men, who, no doubt, will assist him in his villanous undertaking : Now, what I have to request of you is only your advice in this emergency.

"You have had much experience in military af-fairs, and as I have now a body of infantry fully in-structed in the English discipline, I would have your instructions how to employ them to the best advantage. I also want your joint advice as to another matter. The rebel chief is now at the head of seventy thousand mal-contents, advancing rapidly to Candahar, with a design to invest that capital, cause himself to be pro-claimed Shah, levy all the force he can there, and ad-vance hither with all speed ; for he expects the reduc-tion of this city will, if effected, seat him quietly on the throne of Persia.—Now, whether is it best to raise a powerful army here, and wait his approach ; or march directly to Candahar, and give him a repulse, at least, at a distance? Speak your sentiments as usual, with freedom ; for let the the final issue be what it may, I am too well convinced of your sincerity to impute the cause of any disaster that may happen, to your advice." Here he paused for a reply.

Augustus delivered his sentiments in the following terms.

" The many and particular marks of distinction
with which my friends and I have been honoured, by
the unbounded liberality of your majesty, as well as the
freedom of speech and action with which we have been
indulged, ever since we were so happy as to find an
asylum within the walls of the monarch of Persia, em-
boldens me to offer my sentiments, on the present occasion, without reserve: Not only so, I will yield all
the personal assistance in my power freely. Dispatch
a courier, immediately, to the Governor of Candahar,
with peremptory orders, to put himself in the best posture of defence possible; to hold himself in readiness to
repulse the rebels, and assure him of speedy and sufficient succours under your immediate command. Let
Casbin be garrisoned and fortified as a check on Asterabat. You have now five thousand troops initiated in
the management of the firelock and bayonet; take two
thousand of those and a sufficient body of cavalry, and
march directly for Candahar. The remaining three
thousand I would keep here to fortify this city and put
every thing in order to give the insurgents a warm reception, if they should reach so far before they are reduced to obedience: Finally, if you find it impossible
to maintain your ground at Candahar, endeavour, by
all means to effect an orderly retreat to this capital, before your troops are thrown into disorder; for depend
on it, if matters are brought to that crisis, your success
will ultimately depend on that manœuvre. Be not too
sanguine; if Candahar holds out until your arrival, it
will strike the insurgents with terror, to see that you

have yet thoufands of faithful fubjects, rallying with courage round the royal ftandard and commanded by their prince in perfon.

" This is, in my opinion, the moft probable method to enfure fuccefs, for the Candahar army, if a retreat is inevitable, will accompany the troops under your command, and, if the retreat is orderly, you will acquire (like a ftream running back on itfelf) additional ftrength and numbers in every mile of your march ; whereas if your forces are put to precipitate flight, 'twill be exactly the reverfe.

" If thefe meafures are purfued, I have not the leaft doubt of your majefty's arms being crowned with glory, the traitor punifhed, and your deluded fubjects returning to their former allegiance." " My invaluable friend," faid Kerim, embracing him, " your words re-animate my foul ! I am determined to purfue your advice.—How happy you would make me if you would accept the command of thofe three thoufand infantry who are to remain in Ifpahan : Your prefence would infpire thofe officers and men (who have been trained to your hand, by your own precepts and under your immediate infpection) with redoubled vigour ; and almoft enfure fuccefs. Under your aufpices they will learn to encounter and defeat the rebellious banditti, who are now meditating a blow, which they intend, fhall overturn all law and order, and introduce anarchy and confufion ; rapine, plunder and bloodfhed."

"That shall never be, while I am able to yield a sword. No, Kerim, I repeat it again, I will not sheathe my sword until your rebellious subjects are reduced to submission, or Augustus Davenport is lying, undistinguishable, among a pile of slain." "And a sword you shall have," said the monarch, in raptures, "worthy of your noble spirit, and the cause you have so generously espoused." He immediately took off his own cimeter, and presented it to Augustus, saying, "Accept this, it has passed from father to son, through four generations, and has never been taken by an enemy, nor sullied by the hand of a coward or traitor; and my reason for transferring it to you, is, a confidence of its being never employed in a dishonorable cause."

He then earnestly solicited the assistance of Charles and Mercutio, and offered them commissions in the first grade; but they refused, and gave for reason, that in the very critical state of his majesty's affairs, their promotion over the heads of numbers of brave and worthy Persians might be productive of jealousy and disgust; particularly in weak and prejudiced minds; but cheerfully offered to serve under Augustus, and to exert all their powers in bringing about a happy reconciliation.

The Sophi was highly satisfied with their friendly offers, and on reflection, could not but approve their resolutions, requested them all to take such measures for the accomplishment of the great object in view as they should judge requisite.

These preliminaries being settled, Kerim issued the
necessary instructions to those Persian officers who
were to remain in Ispahan, in order to co-operate with
Augustus, and his friends; then, taking an affectionate
leave of them all, set out at the head of his army for
Candahar, amidst the tears, prayers and acclamations
of his people, of every description.—Augustus immediately convened the principal officers, in order to consult on the steps, necessary to be first taken, to render
the city tenable, against any force that might be brought
against it. The result of this conference was, that Augustus should take on him the chief command of both
infantry and cavalry (the latter he peremptorily refused,
but was obliged to appoint the commander; he pitched
on a noble and brave officer, nephew to the Sophi,
named Azounkar.) Mercutio and Charles as lieuten-
ant generals.

Augustus immediately divided his troops into three
bodies of a thousand each; Augustus commanded one,
Mercutio and Charles the other two. The two latter
to form ambuscades on the wings of the city at the distance of one hundred fathoms in advance, from the
two extreme angles of the city walls, in front, and six
hundred fathoms from each other, exactly opposite.
Intrenchments were immediately thrown up to cover
the ambuscades, who were not to discover themselves
until a concerted signal was given from the top of the
city walls; then to flank, and, if possible, surround the
enemy, who being galled in front from the walls, would
give ground, which would throw the rear into confu-

son, and while turning to fly, and finding an enemy behind, would become desperate, and the engagement in consequence become general and decisive.

A body of five thousand choice cavalry was dispatched to Casbin, and as many more to secure a communication between that city and the capital: Small parties of horse were kept in continual motion, and in every possible direction, particularly towards Candahar.

Thus, having taken every precaution which appeared necessary, and laid every thing in as proper a train as time and circumstances would admit, they anxiously waited the event.

On the seventh day after the royal army began its march towards Candahar, two spies were brought in by a scouting party, who, after informing Augustus that the rebels to the number of one hundred thousand, had closely invested Candahar, and that they were sure that city must fall into their hands, were hanged without the walls.

In the evening of the next day, arrived thirty thousand horse from the provinces of Kirman and Chusistan: These troops were refreshed, and being divided, were encamped on the outward wings of the ambuscades, in order to sustain the first onset of the insurgents; then to make a show of retreating to the city gates, but when within one hundred fathoms, to divide in good order,

and retire to the right and left, through the two chafms
between the walls and the ambufcades.

At this critical moment the gates were to be thrown
open, and Auguftus with his corps to march out,
form in a folid column, advance within a few paces,
fire right in the face of the enemy, and rufh on them
with fixed bayonets: In this ftage of the conflict, the
fignal for the ambufcades to appear was to be hoifted.

The next day, a courier arrived, with difpatches
from Kerini, fignifying that the infurgents had taken
poffeffion of Candahar before he could poffibly reach it;
that he had fuftained confiderable lofs in an engagement
with a large detachment of the rebel army, and was
then retreating in good order, and expected to be at
the gates of Ifpahan in a few days; adding, that the rebel chief had drawn out his whole force, to purfue him,
faid to confift of one hundred and thirty thoufand ef-
fective men; and that though Candahar had furrendered to fuperior numbers, they only waited a favorable
opportunity to flock to the ftandard of their lawful fovereign.

Broken parties of cavalry were continually flocking
in, after this intelligence, fome bringing a few prifoners, and fome accompanied by deferters; but all concurred in the account of the total defeat of the royal army and of the taking of the Sophi, who was fent a pri-

foner to Candahar, and that the enemy purfued the
fhattered remains of his army with all poffible fpeed.

It feems the Sophi's army having been preffed hard
for four days and nights, continually galled in flank
and harraffed in rear, was conftrained to halt, (not
encamp) for a few hours repofe: Hunger and fatigue,
the harbingers of difcontent and lownefs of fpirits, prevented them from taking the neceffary precautions for
their fafety: The confequence was, they were furrounded in the night, and almoft all cut off, and Kerim,
with feveral of his officers made prifoners.

A council was called, in confequence of this information, confifting of all the principal officers, civil as
well as military, wherein it was refolved not to make
any alteration in the prefent difpofition of the troops ;
to difpatch expreffes to each of the provinces, yet in
Kerim's intereft, requefting fpeedy fuccours ; at the
fame time, keeping the account laft received a profound
fecret. It was alfo further agreed to admit and keep
all the fcattered forces that might come in before the
arrival of the enemy, within the walls, to be refrefhed
and formed into a corps-de-referve, to act as opportunity or neceffity might require ; and, finally, never to
furrender, but preferve the capital, or fall with their
fwords in their hands.

Thefe preliminaries being adjufted, and the different
difpatches gone, the commanders joined their refpective

corps, in order to wait the approach of the rebels, who, by undoubted information, were actually within forty miles, and advancing rapidly.

At the close of that day, about four hundred of the Sophi's infantry with two thousand horse arrived, who reported that the insurgents, would certainly attack them by day-light next morning ; as their motion had more the appearance of a retreat than an advance. These troops were received into the city for the purpose beforementioned, and two thousand cavalry sent as an advance guard, about seven miles from the city. In the course of that night thirteen thousand cavalry, and two thousand archers arrived from Sableftan : The archers were posted on the walls, and the cavalry took their stand in a wood, within one mile of the city, eastward, in a most advantageous situation; this body of horse, had positive orders not to appear until they saw the insurgents nearly encircled ; then to divide into parties of one hundred men each, advance and dispose themselves in such a manner, that if any part of the enemy's forces should make or attempt a desperate retreat, there should not be left to them even a possibility of an escape.

The sun, just above the horizon, discovered the advanced guard returning with some precipitation, yet in good order; and in a short time, the insurgents, in great force, under a thick cloud of dust, seemed to overspread the whole plain.

A skirmish ensued between the Sophi's cavalry, posted on the wings, and the advance of the rebel army, in which there were but five killed or wounded. The main body of the insurgents now coming up, confident of success from the superiority of their numbers; the royal cavalry, as preconcerted, retreated towards the city, pursued briskly by the rebels, who concluded all was their own; but the Sophi's horse retreating to the right and left, they advanced within sixty fathoms, and, by a flag, demanded an immediate surrender, on pain of indiscriminate carnage. This was peremptorily refused, in consequence of which, the rebel chief ordered to advance to the very gates.

When they were within musquet shot, the gates flew open, Augustus with his infantry sallied forth, and instantly formed in a solid column. The appearance of this column disconcerted them for a moment; but, confiding in the superiority of their numbers, they advanced rapidly, thinking to trample them to pieces, at the same time they uttered a shout which rent the air.

It is impossible to describe the consternation of the insurgents, when their whole front fell at the first fire of the column.———Barbarossa, the rebel chief, notwithstanding this disaster, led on his men a second time to the charge: Now the archers, from the walls discharged a cloud of arrows full in their faces, under cover of which the infantry advanced with secured bayonets, which threw them into inconceivable confusion.

The signal for the ambuscades being displayed in this moment of dread and surprize, the rebels were immediately surrounded, and assaulted on all sides, they fell like leaves in autumn, to attempt a retreat or rally, being equally vain, their chief hastened to the rear, to encourage his unhappy adherents by his presence; he was, however, intercepted in his way by Mercutio, who, dexterously shunning a lance aimed at him by Barbarossa, plunged his sword to the hilt in his left side, and he fell, with his horse, which that instant received a bullet in the head.

The wretched rebels seeing themselves environed on every side, and their leader slain, grew desperate, and for some time fought like so many furies; but in vain did they attempt to penetrate the columns of infantry; they fell like grass before the scythe; the arrows of the archers, and the pointed bayonets bid defiance to their numerous squadrons.

At length, seeing nothing but death before and danger behind, they threw down their arms and sued for quarter: This was granted, and an immediate stop put to the carnage, which was dreadful: The field was in many places, not only strewed with dead and wounded, but man and horse, some dead, some dying, some slightly wounded, swords and broken lances were thrown, as it were, promiscuously together, in heaps, to the terror and astonishment of the survivors.

After securing the prisoners, &c. they found their loss in killed and wounded amounted to something more than four hundred foot, and two thousand horse, including officers, several of whom were of the first rank. Fifteen thousand of the insurgents lay dead on the field ; the wounded amounted to a still greater number, the greater part of whom died of their wounds, whether for want of skill or diligence is not known : The weather being exrremely sultry, perhaps contibuted, in a great measure, to gangrene their wounds, and thereby retard, at least, if not entirely prevent the cure.

It was next resolved in a council of war, that Augustus should remain at Ispahan with one thousand infantry and twelve thousand horse ; while Mercutio and Charles should march the remainder of the troops, horse and foot to Candahar, in order to release the Sophi, and reduce the remainder of the mal-contents to obedience.

The troops destined for Candahar, encamped without the late field of battle, in order to refresh ; while those who were to remain were employed in burying the dead, and in removing the wounded to places appointed for their reception, without the walls.

In two days, the troops being thoroughly refreshed and fit for action, the Candahar detachment marched under the auspices of Mercutio, Charles and several Persian commanders of great bravery.

The infantry, in two columns, were led by Mercutio and Charles, the archers on the wings: Six thousand cavalry formed the advance, four thousand on each flank, seven thousand more closed the rear, and five hundred were formed into ten scouting parties, fifty men in each, to scour the country.

They arrived before Candahar in the night; and seizing the out guards, suddenly and without noise, secured them, and rushed into the city pell-mell, before the inhabitants or troops of the garrison were apprized of their situation.

The streets were instantly lined with armed men, the keys of the gates were secured, a strong guard environed the Governor's palace and treasury, and the Sophi's guards were placed as centinels in every avenue.

A message was immediately dispatched to the Governor, informing him of the change of affairs, accompanied with a demand of the person of the Sophi immediately; to which was added, a threat to put all to the sword, without respect to age, sex or denomination, in case of any hesitation or refusal.

The meffenger returned in a very fhort time, with an invitation to the commander in chief, from the Sophi, requefting an interview at the Governor's palace.

Now there being no fuch commander, Mercutio and Charles infifted ftrongly, at firft, on Kerim's nephew to appear in that character, as he was commander in chief of the cavalry; but this he refufed, fo that at length, by the joint folicitations of all the reft of the officers, Mercutio was prevailed on to go. He was met at the gate of the palace by Kerim the Governor and moft of the principal men of the province.

"Welcome, thrice welcome," faid Kerim, to our hero, "my dear friend! My brother! Preferver of my life! Thanks to the eternal Alla for the prefervation of my friend. Where are our other friends? Is my fon fafe?" Our hero, in as concife a manner as the nature of the fubject would admit, informed him of the lateft occurrences at Ifpahan; the real ftate of his affairs in that quarter, and of the welfare of his fon and other friends.

Kerim expreffed his fatisfaction in the moft animated language, while the ftrong expreffion of his countenance difplayed the grateful fenfations of his heart.

The reft of the principal officers were next fent for, who foon appeared before their beloved fovereign, and manifefted the moft unfeigned fatisfaction on his reftora-

tion. They, each in his turn congratulated him on the
fuccefs of his arms. The Perfian commanders attribut-
ed the late victory folely to the valour and difcipline of
the legion of infantry ; and affured his majefty that the
royal cavalry muft inevitably have been routed, had it
not been for the judicious difpofitions, planned by the
fuperior fkill of Auguftus and his colleagues.

" My worthy friends," faid Kerim, " Ever fince
the event which gave birth to our friendfhip I have fenfibly felt the weight of the obligations under which
your generofity has laid me ; but now I defpair of ever
having it in my power to make any compenfation that
will bear the fmalleft proportion to the accumulated
load : The life and education of my fon—My own life,
my honour, and my Empire ; all thefe do I owe to
your wifdom and valour—But why fhould I recount
particulars ? Lives there a loyal fubject of mine who
is not indebted to you for the freedom he this day en-
joys ? But no more of this—I know your generous
difinterefted difpofitions, and will therefore fupprefs
thofe effuffions, and wave the converfation.

" Let us fet our affairs in order here, and return to
Ifpahan. I am anxious to embrace our dear Auguftus—To fold my dear Abbafs to this breaft, in all the
ecftacy of parental affection. Come my friends, I am
conftrained by the urgency of my affairs, to folicit
your advice once more.

The revolted provinces are at present in a state of the utmost confusion; order must be re-established before we can pretend to sit down satisfied. Chorazan is at present without a Governor, consequently discord, cruelty, rapine and oppression reign uncontrouled, the reduction of this province to order, demands our first and principal attention.

"Having given me such powerful assistance you will not, I trust, desert me until, we have secured the fruit of our labours, beyond a possibility of its being wrested from our hands; to restore peace and its attendent blessings to my subjects, and to prevent the further effusion of blood, is our ultimate wish: In order to facilitate this so desirable an undertaking, I request your advice; as I freely confess my self embarrassed, and much at a loss where to begin."

After a long consultation, it was finally determined that Azounkar, should march the cavalry under his command, with the addition of one thousand infantry, invested with all the powers necessary to take possession of the governmental reins, in the room and stead of the traitor Barbarossa, and to proclaim through that province free pardon to all such as had been active in the late rebellion, on condition of a peaceable return to their respective abodes by a certain day, and future good behaviour; otherwise to be put to death as soon as found, without ceremony.

Order being re-eſtabliſhed in Candahar, Azounkar prepared for his march, and after taking an affectionate leave of his uncle and his brother officers, who expreſſed much regret at parting with him, he being no leſs an amiable companion than a valiant commander, he marched under a diſcharge of all the ſmall arms.

The next day Kerim, with his friends, Mercutio and Charles, ſet out for the capital of the Perſian Empire. They were met within two leagues of the walls, by the loyal inhabitants of that city, with Auguſtus and Abbaſs at their head. Nothing could exceed the joy of Abbaſs, on ſeeing and embracing his royal father in peace and ſafety. The loyal citizens, after having congratulated their ſovereign on his ſucceſs, accompanied him to the palace; then diſperſed with every mark of ſatisfaction, to their reſpective places of abode.

The troops were encamped without the walls, and four days were ſpent in public rejoicing: The troops were feaſted ſumptuouſly and Kerim diſtributed, with his own hands, an equal donation to each ſoldier.

The day being arrived for the departure of the troops drawn from the diſtant provinces, they marched, full of grateful acknowledgements of the liberality of their ſovereign, whoſe approbation crowned their victory with happineſs, and added freſh verdure to their laurels.

Abbaſs, who had not left Auguſtus from the time his father marched from Candahar, until his return, but, having attended to every plan laid down, and every order given by him, with the utmost avidity, it is not to be wondered at, if he made a very great improvement in the military art: This was the case, in consequence of which, Kerim was transported almost to enthusiasm. He could not forbear expressing his gratitude in words as well as actions. He considered his three friends as the saviours of his life and restorers of his Empire; he would have loaded them with the most precious treasures of the East: In short, he wished to spend his days with them, and to that end would have sacrificed the half of his dominions to have retained them in Persia.

But the period was fast advancing which was to separate those sincere friends; Mercutio and Isabella both grew impatient, and panted for the attainment of that goal which they had figured to themselves, as the ultimate point of their pursuit.

After several private consultations held on the subject of their intended route, our hero and his friends determined on passing through the Russian territories as the safest, and, perhaps, most expeditious.

When Kerim was apprized of their design of setting off in the course of ten days at farthest, he changed colour, and pensively said: "So then we must part at " last! Has heaven raised me to this exalted pinnacle " of happiness, with no other design than to teach me

" submission, by plunging me suddenly into impenetra-
" ble solitude? Oh that I could devise means to ren-
" der any part of the Empire of Persia sufficiently
" agreeable to them, to become their permanent resi-
" dence! Then I might be said to be truly happy—To
" enjoy the sweets of unadulterated friendship."

Then, as if suddenly recollecting himself: " But
why this ungenerous wish, this selfish desire? What
strange unaccountable beings does this self-love make
of us! The supposed object of our love we rule with the
most tyrannical sway; and at the very moment we
profess the most ardent passion for, we wish to prevent
the lawful pursuits and even to shackle the very ideas of
that object. Shall self-love dissolve the ties of sacred
friendship? by no means. Mercutio has taught me to
meet misfortunes with becoming fortitude; and disap-
pointments with reverential submission; then I will endeavour to bid them adieu with cheerfulness. Why should
they forego their own pleasure to promote mine? Away
with such ungenerous sentiments! Am not I indebted
to them for all my present possessions? Have they not
freely hazarded their lives in my defence!"

After a short pause: " A pang, however, in de-
spite of reason and rectitude, will intrude in the parting moment: I already anticipate it, but must yield.

" Let them know," said he to Abbass, to whom
the foregoing was addressed, " that I assent cheerfully,

that I defire our correfpondence may be as heretofore, unreftrained, and that during the fhort, very fhort remaining interval, the circumftance of their departure be not fo much as mentioned until the evening preceding: Difagreeable tidings are ever premature.——Let us fpend this evening in our garden of Tzarbach"*

The evening was fpent, as might have been expected, in that kind of rational, fubftantial pleafure, which nought but unaffected fincerity can convey, and real friendfhip experience. Abbafs, Ifabella and Mercutio retired fometime before the reft of the company, who remained in Tzarbach till very late. They proceeded flowly to the palace by the light of the moon. The So-

* This is one of the moft beautiful gardens in the Perfian Empire, and perhaps in the whole world. It is one league and a half fquare, contrived in fuch a manner, that the fmall river Senderuth, divides it into four exact fquares, or quarters; each of which is under the higheft ftate of cultivation, managed by no lefs than twenty-five gardeners of exquifite tafte and fkill, to each fquare. In the centre of the whole, is a bafon of white marble; from the centre of which, a large column of water is projected to the height of forty feet. At the corner of each fquare (next the fountain) ftands a moft fuperb pavillion; the apartments, decorated with curious carved work, richly gilt and furnifhed. Every avenue in this fpacious garden is accommodated with a leffer bafon of marble, which is exceedingly refrefhing; and the oloriferous plants with which the walks are lined, diffufe a fragrance over the whole, which is abfolutely indefcribable, and the medicinal plants and herbs every where difperfed, baffle both defcription and calculation.

phi leading the way, conducted them through a long avenue, which was terminated by a flight of marble steps, which led to the Harem. Kerim determined to surprize Charles and Augustus, with a sight both novel and unexpected ; accordingly, in consequence of a preconcerted signal, given by the Sophi, (a stamp with his foot) the folding doors flew open, and discovered thirty and seven females of different nations, religions, sizes, features and complexions, arrayed in all the pomp of magnificent prostitution.

The apartment was illuminated so as to form an artificial day ; But not a motion was made, nor a word spoke, until a nod from Kerim gave birth to a most delightful vocal concert. It was those females who had so frequently contributed to their satisfaction before, though unseen.

Many a side long glance was stolen by some of those hapless females, at their new visitors ; who, on the other hand, found employment for both eyes and ears: They had now an opportunity which they had never met, nor in all human probability ever were likely to meet again, that of observing the gestures and emotions of this collection of females, some of whom where retained by compulsion, some were perfectly pleased with their situation ; while others appeared overwhelmed with a kind of stupor, and totally insensible of the wretchedness of their condition.

There were to be found among them, the prude, the coquette; some who were perfectly adepts in the art of pleasing (a very necessary ingredient in the composition of a woman) and all, except two, in that of dissimulation: These two, very soon fixed the attention of Charles and Augustus; who each, unknown to the other, resolved if possible, to inform themselves of their former circumstances and situations, as well as the vicissitudes which had reduced them to the present.

The concert ended, they took leave of the Sophi and retired to rest.

When they had reached their apartment, said Charles, " I do not wonder that Kerim complains of the want of sincerity among his courtiers, and others who surround his person, when I reflect on the abject situation of all his subjects. They are slaves in effect; for was the throne of Persia occupied by a monarch of vicious principles (which Kerim is not) they would be completely wretched. Yet they live happy, and I may add free, merely owing to the natural goodness of his heart. He has beauties here under his roof, who no doubt possess every qualification necessary to render him happy, if he could but be convinced of the propriety of being attached to one alone: But alas! Sensual gratification, and variety, comprehend the sum of his enjoyment in that quarter.

I perceived, this evening, in the countenances of some of those ill-fated creatures, a mixture of reluctance and remorse in their apparent endeavours to please the Sophi and us. Did you not observe the two who sat opposite to us, and under the mark of serenity, betrayed symptoms of latent grief (if I mistake not) and when observed, were certainly much embarrassed?" "I did," replied Augustus, "and though arbitrary power, under whatever form, was ever my bane, my aversion to it, is this evening increased in a ten fold proportion. There appeared, to me, something in the air of the two you mention, superior to the rest, and deserving of a better fate; and I am anxious, I know not why, to learn something of their history. I am inclined to think they have, like ourselves, been unfortunate, and brought here by force, and having no friend to assist or ransom them, are compelled to linger out the residue of their days in silent misery, divested of every comfort in this life, except a participation of each others woes in private."

"You have exactly expressed my sentiments: I am resolved to consult Mercutio to-morrow, on the means most proper to be employed, in order to obtain the desired information."

The next day they acquainted Mercutio with the prededing night's adventure, and their remarks thereon, which very much excited his curiosity, and he regretted his not being present.

They agreed to use their mutual endeavours to convince the Sophi of the absurdity of expecting, and the impossibility of finding that pleasure (which is the ultimate end of every rational connexion between the sexes) in an alternate cohabitation with a large plurality of women, such as have been already described ; and to point out the palpable advantages, as well as pleasures, that would necessarily result from his making choice of one female, with whom he might share his bed and throne, his joys and cares ; and thus to eradicate, if possible, those mistaken ideas, which national prejudice and the force of education, had implanted in his breast ; and which, as a false mirror, represented every object in a wrong point of view, and consequently mislead his judgment.

This day, a very singular scene presented itself, which had a most powerful tendency to promote their intended conversion of the Sophi, in awakening the feelings of Kerim ; in opening his heart to the dictates of justice and in interesting his affections in the cause of oppressed innocence :—An ancient couple, natives of the province of Chorazan, appeared at the gate of the palace, where, meeting Mercutio, they applied to him to procure them admission into the presence of the Sophi.

He immediately acquainted his majesty with the request of the applicants, who desiring to see them, our hero conducted them in.

The venerable pair immediately proftrated themfelves
before Kerim, and burft into tears. The Sophi ordered them to rife and inform him of the caufe of their
emotion. They obeyed, and the man, after a fhort
paufe, addreffed the monarch in the following terms:

" Moft gracious Kerim! You now behold before
you a man who has wafted the prime of his youth, and
ftrength of his manhood, in defence and fupport of the
royal throne of Perfia. The fincerity of my attachment to the intereft of your royal father, is not altogether unknown to you, oh Kerim!

" When worn down with age, and unable to render
any further fervice to my prince and country in the
field, I retired to the province of my nativity, in order
to fpend the refidue of my days on my own paternal
eftate.—I drank large draughts of happinefs in the endearing company and converfation of my dear Zobeide,
and one dear child—a daughter."—Tears, in rapid
fucceffion, defcended down his venerable cheeks—he
recovered—" Gracious Prince!" he exclaimed, " pardon the weaknefs of a poor old man, an unfortunate
father!

" When the rebel Barbaroffa, caufed himfelf to be pro-
claimed Shah of Perfia, I abhorring fuch rebellious
proceedings, refufed my affent and affiftance at his
mock inauguration; which has brought down his ven-

geance on my devoted head, and has completely defo-
lated my late small but happy family.

"In order to prevent some of the intended effects of
this most unnatural rebellion, I immediately wrote to
thee, Oh Kerim, a letter containing a minute description of the face of affairs in Chorazan, that you
might have it in your power to avoid the impend-
ing storm."

"Gracious Alla! exclaimed the Sophi—" art thou
Mahumed?" "The very same," replied the old man.
Kerim embraced him with ardor. "Welcome, re-
nowned Mahumed art thou to me—But I interrupt
thee, proceed."

"A traitor from your royal court, an emissary from
Barbarossa, who was here when the letter arrived, and
contrived to inform himself of the general contents,
pursued my servant, and seizing him suddenly, bound
him on a camel, and straightway conveyed him to the
rebel chief, who tortured him in the most cruel manner,
in order to extort a discovery of the person who had
wrote the letter; but without effect: The faithful
creature, chose rather to expire under the most excruciating torments (which he finally did) than betray a
master who had placed a confidence in him, and whom
he loved as a father.

" The well known attachment I had ever manifested
to the royal house of Shah Kerim, was no secret to
Barbarossa.   He fixed his suspicion on me, and determined to ruin me at all events.

" Aware of my being universally known and respected, by all the inhabitants of Herat; he coward-like
resolved to prosecute his revenge privately.

" One evening, returning from the Mosque to my
house, I received a stroke on the temple which laid
me senseless on the ground.

" How long I remained in this situation, or how I was
treated until I recovered my senses, I know not.   I
found myself immured in a humid, dark and noisome
dungeon.   I received as much rice and water as supported life, but heard not the human voice; nor saw
the light of day, until the arrival of Azounkar: But
neither the want of light, food or liberty were held in
any competition by me, with the dreadful mortification
I endured in being deprived of the consolating company
of my dear Zobeide, and that of my enchanting Zayde,
the only pledge of our reciprocal affection.   All this,
however, was felicity, compared with the agony of
mind which I have constantly endured ever since I was
liberated.

" In the same hour that I was seized, a posse of rebels surrounded my house, and, after stopping the

mouth of my dear Zobeide, ftript it of every thing valuable, and, oh torture! my lovely Zayde! ever fince my liberation I have been feeking her, and but two days ago was informed, that when the rebels were overthrown, fhe was taken by Solim Abbafi (the atrocious villain who took my fervant, and was the caufe of all the mifery I ever experienced) to the diftant province of Adribeitzan, where he has a number of friends.

" I know her foul is rent with anguifh, if even nothing worfe than our feparation has taken place, and the diftance is fo great, that, fatigued as we are, it is next to impoffible for us to perform the journey, and if we even could, it is more than probable the villain would find means to elude our vigilance, or, if found, would perhaps but infult our mifery.

" This O Kerim! is the fum of my diftrefs, and, confiding in your well known benevolence and juftice, I have prefumed to lay my grievances before you, in full affurance of obtaining redrefs."

" Yes," faid the monarch, " and ample redrefs you fhall have." He then gave orders to a vigilant officer, to march with a company of horfe, immediately, and to bring Selim Abbafi, with all his houfhold, to Ifpahan, with all poffible fpeed.

" Mahumed," faid he, " you will remain in our palace until they return, you fhall be accommodated with every thing neceſſary while you ſtay here, and when you chooſe to depart, I will reward your loyalty, by rendering you as affluent as you were before this misfortune happened ; and if you have a mind to ſpend the remainder of your days in Iſpahan, I will eſtabliſh you to your ſatisfaction—you ſhall ever have a particular place in my eſteem : In the mean time, make yourſelf as eaſy as poſſible, matters may not be ſo deſperate as they appear ; your daughter may yet be reſtored to you in ſafety."

The conference broke up, and Kerim gave orders to his chief Eunuch, to accommodate the venerable Mahumed in the beſt manner poſſible.

The Sophi propoſed a turn in the garden, Mercutio and his friends followed. The diſcourſe turned on the diſtreſſes of Mahumed. Kerim reprobated, in the ſtrongeſt terms, the proceedings of the traitorous villain, who had been the cauſe of them, and ſympathetically deplored his loſs of property ; but expreſſed no concern about that of his daughter, nor about the probable conſequences of her being forced away by an abominable ſcoundrel, who would ſtick at nothing to obtain the gratification of his luſt and revenge : So prevalent is the idea of compulſion with regard to females among the votaries of Mahomet, that their conſent to the will of their tyrants is never thought of, much leſs ſought.

Mercutio took this opportunity of expatiating largely on the abfurdity, as well as injuftice, of forcing the inclinations of a woman. "Your majefty is fully fenfible, that if a man is not faithful to his prince by inclination, it is morally impoffible to fecure his fidelity by force: It is true, he may be compelled to render fome fervices, however contrary to his will; but even thefe will inevitably ceafe, whenever a relaxation of the compulfive power occurs. How widely different are the fervices fo extorted, from thofe which flow from a fincere defire to pleafe; which are performed voluntarily, void of any kind of compulfion or reftraint."

"Your obfervation is certainly juft," replied the Sophi, "but I am not convinced that the fimile will equally apply to females; however, we will difcourfe further on the fubject this evening, and if you can by pure dint of reafon, demonftrate the impropriety of a cuftom fo long, and fo univerfally eftablifhed in all the eaftern nations, I fhall readily fubmit."

In the evening, Auguftus hinted to the Sophi, the defire of Mercutio to be admitted into the Harem. "His curiofity fhall be gratified," faid he, "for I neither can nor will refufe him any favor in my power to grant." They were juft then joined by Mercutio and Charles. "Well, my friends," faid Kerim, "I am glad of your company, at this time particularly, as I feel anxious to renew the converfation with Mer-

K

cutio: My mind has been exercifed, fince morning, in an unufual manner, feveral circumftances have been prefented to my imagination, which never exifted there before, and which I wifh to have placed in proper points of view; but we will defer the matter until Abbafs, (who rode without the walls for exercife,) returns, in order that he may improve by our converfation: In the interim, I will introduce you into my Harem, Mercutio has never feen the variety of beauties which it contains, neither has any man ever been admitted, myfelf and the Eunuchs who have the care of the women, excepted."

He then conducted them into his repofitory of female flaves, who in a fhort time made their appearance, and having received their inftructions from the Eunuch, who introduced them, began to fing as before.

Mercutio and his friends paid very little attention to the harmony, they remarked the countenances of the whole, and Mercutio very readily diftinguifhed the two who had been fo particularly noted by his friends before.

The Sophi at length gave the females a fignal to withdraw, after which he afked Mercutio his opinion of the performance, and beauty of his women, who anfwered, that, in his judgment, their voices were exceedingly melodious, and their perfons, generally, were not inferior to any that had come under his obfervation in any country.

The evening being remarkably fine, the Sophi propofed fpending an hour or two in the gardens, where they were foon joined by Abbafs, who informed his father, that he had juft received a letter from his kinfman, Azounkar: By this they learnt that the daughter of Mahumed had juft returned to Herat, and after having ufed her utmoft diligence to difcover the retreat of her parents, without fuccefs, had applied to him for intelligence, and finding he was not able to give any account of them, fhe was on the point of deftroying herfelf, but was prevented. When her phrenzy had fubfided, he interrogated her concerning thofe violent emotions; fhe related the circumftances of her having been feized and torn from the arms of her mother, by Selim Abbafi, adding, that fhe had been conveyed to a great diftance, on horfeback, furrounded entirely by armed horfemen; and that fhe had been kept a clofe prifoner ever fince, until fome days ago, when fhe had the good fortune to efcape from her confinement.

This villain having repeatedly attempted to win her to his embraces, fometimes by flattery, at others by threats, and finding all his art infufficient to procure the gratification of his luft, he at length determined on force, and with that intent entered the room where fhe was confined. Finding her averfion ftronger than ever, drew a dagger from his fafh, fwearing by Mahomet, if she resisted his will any longer, he would sheathe it in her heart. The sense of her unhappy situation deprived her of reason for some time. When she recovered, she burst into tears and he taking advantage of her confusion, seized her in his arms and carried her to a couch, in spite of her struggles, in order to accomplish his vile purpose by main force, and would certainly have succeeded, had not her eye caught the dagger, and, believing her ruin inevitable, resolutely seized and plunged it into his heart. Half distracted with grief and horror, she arose, and with the reeking instrument of death in her hand, resolved to explore a passage, or sacrifice her life in the attempt. She was met on the stair-case by an old Eunuch, who had been her jailer, he attempted to intercept her flight; but she fearless as the tygress, gave him a mortal wound, as she supposed, and left him in the same grovelling posture, with his infamous master: Then pressing towards the outer door, she opened it and rushed forth, penetrated with all the horrors which such a train of circumstances must have naturally inspired.

Mere accident, as it should seem, directed her into the direct road to Herat, and after a few days, arrived in her native city, sorely fatigued, and under great depression of spirits.

He further added, that it appeared to him likely, that Mahumed would shape his course for Ispahan, and, if that should be the case, requested his uncle to cause the earliest intelligence to be transmitted to him, as he was apprehensive his daughter would take some opportunity to end her days by violent means, if she did not hear some news of her parents very shortly.

"Gracious Alla!" exclaimed Kerim, "what an atrocious villain has here met his just reward! a villain of the most unjust and obdurate kind! who, so far from being content with the ruin of that honorable and virtuous character, her father, would have imbrued his hands in the blood of his innocent, unoffending daughter, merely for refusing the embraces of her father's mortal enemy."

Mahumed was then sent for, and the welcome tidings of his daughter announced to him.

"Thanks to the immortal Alla! exclaimed he in extasy: Thou hast been graciously pleased to hear and grant the ardent desires of my heart, which I have unceasingly poured out before thee, for the preservation of a dear and only child, ever since she has been so cruelly separated from my protecting arms! Blessings attend the noble Azounkar! May the immortal Prophet, whom all the faithful continually serve, shower down his choicest blessings on the head of the benevolent, the beloved Kerim! With a heart distended with joy and gratitude, I will now take my departure from Ispahan. My beloved Zobeide is yet ignorant of the joyful information.—I hasten to remove the load of distress which sorely oppress the tenderest of bosoms.

"To-morrow we will set out for Herat; I already anticipate the renewed pleasure of clasping my dear Zayde to this breast, and of intermingling, with hers, my tears of joy. May Kerim live and reign, long and happily over a loyal people! And when it shall please the great Alla, to translate him to those regions of eternal felicity, which he has appointed for the reception of the virtuous, mayest thou, O Abbass! dignify the Persian diadem, by acts of benevolence and virtue: The scourge and terror of traitors; and the boast and glory of every loyal Persian!"

Thus, the venerable Mahumed, fraught with loyalty and gratitude, and on the impatient wing of expectation, was on the point of setting out on the instant, had not the Sophi prevented him. "Mahumed," said Kerim, "you must not leave us thus. Your loyal services rendered to our whole house, as well as your undeviating rectitude of conduct in private life, are not, cannot be forgotten: A sure, though late, reward awaits your fidelity.

"The journey to Herat is long and toilsome, and I wish to see your daughter restored to you, I will dispatch a faithful servant to our beloved kinsman Azounkar, with our orders to receive and conduct her hither with speed and safety, she will be here in much less time than it would take you to go there. Go comfort thy Zobeide, and abide with us until thy daughter arrives: Thou shalt experience that regard which thy noble actions have merited."

The venerable Persian, overwhelmed with a sense of the Sophi's munificence, was unable to reply for some minutes, then, as if recovering from a lethargy, exclaimed "Yes, generous Kerim! Soul of thy illustrious predecessor! I am resolved, if my daughter is restored, I will remain in Ispahan until the angel of death shall press his chilling finger on my eye-lids.—I haste to inform my beloved Zobeide of the safety of her child."

When Mahumed had withdrawn, Kerim was very liberal of his encomiums on the great actions, and invincible fidelity of the good old man, and expressed much satisfaction at having prevailed on him to remain in Ispahan. He immediately issued the necessary orders, for the express to Herat: This commission was given to a well tried officer, whose honour was undoubted. "What," said Kerim to Mercutio, "do you think of the conduct of this old man's daughter?" "I think she acted perfectly right," replied our hero, "for there was no alternative; her life, or what was of infinitely more consequence, her virtue, was at stake; and, had she acted otherwise, one or the other she must have surrendered; but by employing the means which were providentially placed within her reach, she bravely preserved both, at the same time that she rid the world of an unfeeling, treacherous villain; and

I am also of opinion, that if half the pains were taken to inftil into the female part of the world, a proper notion of chaftity, and a nice fenfe of female delicacy, as there are to implant in the minds of the other fex the moft exalted ideas of military valour, female fortitude would become formidable, feduction more difficult, and, confequently, lefs frequent.

"I know," continued he, "that local prejudices are hard to furmount, which is a very weighty obftacle to the acceptation of any principles, however liberal, if confidered as oppofing thofe prejudices. It is next to impoffible, for a perfon bred in a land of univerfal liberty, where every idea of arbitrary power, or conftraint of lawful, rational inclination is obliterated as foon as conceived, to convey a juft fenfe of the proprity of the cuftoms of his own country, into the mind of a perfon, whofe whole mode of education has been calculated to infpire him with fentiments diametrically oppofite; whofe political creed is (by the mere force of education, for no man in a flate of nature ever entertained fuch ideas) uncontrouled dominion and freedom of fpeech and fentiment to the very few, who by hereditary fuccefs or conqueft, acquire power; and the moft implicit obedience and abject fubmiffion of opinion in the many, who are too weak or too fervile, to oppofe fuch an unjuft and unreafonable cuftom.

"Let us for a moment advert to firft principles, that is, let us take a view of man in his natural flate. Here

we find him perfectly free in the exercife of all his faculties, mental and corporal: The great author of
his exiftence himfelf, has impofed no conftraint on
any of his thoughts, words or actions, but fuch as are
unreafonable, unjuft and ungenerous, all which muft
have a tendency to deftroy his own happinefs.   Hence
we muft fee and acknowledge that the principal defign of the Creator in calling man into exiftence, was to
render him happy: This is fufficiently proved by his
permitting him to employ all lawful, and rational
means, in the fearching for and fecuring it ; and pro-
hibiting the performance of any and every action which
might in its confequences obftruct him in the purfuit.

"As it is impoffible to divide or feparate the human
fpecies, without deftroying the whole vifible creation,
we muft naturally infer, that woman was invefted with
the fame, or fimilar privileges, and, being palpably
intended for an affiftant (not flave) to man, in the
prefervation of the fpecies, and in procuring the neceffaries of life ; moft undoubtedly was defigned to
be a partaker with him in that happinefs, which the
Creator allotted him, and on the fame conditions ;
this granted, it is clear, that no power on earth has
a right to deprive her of thofe privileges fo long as fhe
remains virtuous, nor to fubject her to the will of any
man, without her own confent.   Would it not be looked on as a moft unfufferable act of tyranny in any prince
or other fupreme power, to enact a law fubjecting the inclination and purfuits of the fubject to the caprice of fuch,

as by ftratagem or force could get him into their power? Would not the whole world combine, and juftly too, to abolifh fuch an abonimable edict? And fhall we, who turn with horror from fuch flagrant injuftice, with re-fpect to one part of the human fpecies, under fanction of a law too, fhall we, I fay, exercife a far more tyran-nical fway over the other, and that the moft beautiful and defencelefs part, and which, if treated with ten-dernefs and juftice, is capable of affording us more pleafure than all the reft of the creation put together? Shall we deprive ourfelves of the moft delightful in-tercourfe on earth, merely in compliance with a vile cuftom, which reduces us to a level with the brute beafts that roam uncontrouled through the flocks and herds, fubjecting all thofe of inferior ftrength to them-felves?"

"My dear friend," faid Kerim, "It was not till very lately that I ever devoted one moment to reflection on this fubject, and until now I never faw it in the point of view wherein you have juftly placed it, and I muft do you the juftice to confefs, that your reafoning has infpired me with fuch a turn of thinking, as I never had before, and, I am firmly of opinion, I never fhould have acquired, had I been deprived the happinefs of feeing you: My conviction is nearly completed, but, do you think there exifts any real difference between a forced embrace, and that which is the refult of mutual confent?"

" As much as between light and darkness ! Your
majesty, no doubt, remembers, that, in a conversation,
you intimated to me your dislike to the disguised con-
straint which you perceived in the behavior of the most
of those who were near your person ; their speeches,
your majesty observed, were studied, and of course dry
and vapid. Your majesty added, that by the double
dealing of theirs, you were deprived of one principal
ingredient in the happiness of life, namely, unrestrained conversation, wherein the sentiments of the heart
are communicated without dissimulation or reserve.

" Your majesty may also remember, that you had
taken much pains to inspire them with necessary confidence, in order to procure that pleasure, which you
found was not to be obtained without.

" The case is similar to the much desired correspondence with the fair sex : It would be just as rational to
attempt to incorporate water with oil, as to expect
sincerity from a woman who knows she is deprived of
her liberty for no other purpose than to minister to the
lusts of one, who so far from entertaining the least regard for her, that independent of the gratification of
his gross, sensual appetite, considers her as scarcely
superior to a quadruped : Instead of a thousand inde-
scribable graces, peculiar to her sex, which, when ju-
diciously employed as auxiliaries, seldom fail to soften
the most unsusceptible hearts, and captivate the greatest
conquerrors : She suppresses every intruding charm ;

not a word, a motion, or even a glance of her eye,
but is calculated to inspire the most disgusting ideas,
carefully avoiding every motion that might have a
contrary effect. Love is not, like youth and beauty, to
be purchased by riches and honours: It must and will
be free, it is incapable of confinement or restraint, and
gathers strength in a tenfold proportion to the opposition of his progress.

" True it is, that even in England, I have known
women, so dazzled by the glare of riches and titles,
that they have surrendered themselves into the arms of
men, whom they heartily despised; who were notwithstanding so blind as to suppose, that it was the
love of their persons which had captivated the affection of their ladies; when the money was the only
object: But I never knew a couple of this description,
but were miserable the rest of their lives. It is morally impossible for a woman to divide her affections
equally between two men; and as much so for a man
to love a plurality of women at the same time, and
as we are more tenacious in matters of this kind than
in any other concernment of life, the bare idea of a di-
vision of that tenderness which is the source and support
of the intercourse between the sexes; and of which nothing less than the undivided whole can satisfy, is sufficient, of itself, to elevate the passions to a degree of
madness, and to destroy every degree of confidence
between the parties.

" It is the height of abfurdity for a man to feize on, and confine a young creature, and to expect her to contribute to his own happinefs without firft rendering her happy, which is only to be done by permitting her to think for herfelf, and act as fhe pleafes ; by convincing her that he loves her for herfelf, and independently of all the reft of her fex ; fuch difinterefted conduct would infpire her with confidence in his fincerity ; that confidence is the bafis of friendfhip will readily be granted ; and that the tranfition from friendfhip to love is eafy, will not be denied.

" If thefe few broken hints were ferioufly examined, all prejudices laid afide, and fair play given to the natural feelings and dictates of common fenfe, the Seraglio of Achmet, would foon be purged of its boafted beauties, and that monarch would enjoy infinitely more pleafure in the converfation of one, who fhould remain voluntarily, than he now does in the forced obfequioufnefs of the numerous female flaves, who wait his nod and defpife him.

" I perceive your drift," faid Kerim ; " you would infinuate that I as well as the Grand Seignior, by divefting myfelf of the prejudice of education, would readily perceive the propriety of adopting a plan of conduct fimilar to that, which, by pointing out its contraft, as you have juft done, and proved to be the moft proper method of fecuring my own happinefs ; great part of which would be derived from a

L

confcioufnefs of having contributed to that of thofe females, who may pant to return to their friends and
country ; and in a firm confidence in the attachment
of fuch as might choofe to remain. But, my dear
friend, you feem not to be fufficiently aware of a circumstance which, under the new eftablifhment, would be
of great moment to me in the realizing thofe fcenes
of blifs which you have pointed in fuch glowing colours.
It might fo happen that all might choofe to depart ;
or if any remained by choice, they might not poffefs
qualifications to fuit me : How am I to proceed in
either of thefe cafes ? You have by removing one
evil introduced another.

'That apparent evil is no obftacle, and, when the
matter is viewed in its proper light, will vanifh inftantly. Only reflect one moment, how many noble families in the Perfian empire would confider, as the
moft fupreme honour that could poffibly be conferred
on them, an alliance with their fovereign. By making a choice of this nature, without the leaft fhadow of
compulfion or arbitrary power, your majefty will effectually fecure all that happinefs which I have been de-
fcribing, and which cannot be obtained by any other
means.

"I yield," faid the noble Kerim. "Your arguments,
though diametrically oppofite to the principles in which
I have been educated, are neverthelefs founded in
reafon and juftice, and cannot fail to enforce convic-

tion when attended to without prejudice, therefore I cannot withhold my acquiescence.

"From this day forward, I shall consider every human being, male and female, as proceeding from the same Omnipotent hand which gave existence to all; and, of course, entitled to the common rights of all. If any or all the females of my Harem desire their dismission, I will not only give orders for their enlargement, but will also furnish them with the necessary means of returning to their respective countries and connections immediately. To-morrow I will begin this work of reformation, a work that will astonish the whole world, and as you, (to Mercutio,) have clearly convinced me of the propriety of such a measure, I request you and your friends to attend, and be witness to the first fruits of that conviction."

"Excellent prince!" exclaimed every voice. "This single act of yours, will immortalize your royal name more than the most glorious victory you ever yet obtained: You have now gained a victory indeed! A victory without bloodshed! A victory over your own passions and prejudices!

"This noble resolution will entail blessings on your royal progeny, will inspire your subjects with (if possible) a still greater reverence for your sacred person, and will establish your majesty in a state of felicity to

which the illiberal and licentious part of mankind
is totally eftranged."

The night being far advanced, they retired to reft,
promifing themfelves abundance of fatisfaction the enfuing day.

The next morning, they found the Sophi uncommonly cheerful, and converfing on the propofed bufinefs of the day; he informed them that the number
of his women was feventeen, natives of almoft as many countries, viz. two from Ruffia, one from Den-
mark, one from Pruffia, two from Spain, two from
France, fix from different provinces of Perfia, one
from Conftantinople and two from England.

"The two laft mentioned," faid he, "I have endeavoured by all the means in my power to infpire
with fentiments agreeable to my own wifhes; but in
vain, and I candidly affure you all, that if it fhould happen to be the choice of either of them to remain here, I
will take her to my arms this day and make her joint
partner in my bed and throne. But I have no hope of
this being the cafe; for a fettled melancholy preys on
their minds, and it feems as if they found a degree of
pleafure in indulging it. However, there is at leaft
a poffibility, that when they are acquainted with my
real wifhes, matters may take a favorable turn.

"I have this morning informed them all by the mouth of my son (I chose to employ him in this busi-ness, in order to impress the circumstance on his mind so as it might not be easily eradicated) of my intentions, and the result is, they all begged to be dismissed ex-cept the lady from Spain and one of the Persians, whom I would willingly dismiss also ; (the two from England believing the whole to be a falsehood, have given no answer.)

"If neither of the English ladies can be prevailed on to accept such offers as I am ready to make, I will send them away and in pursuance of your advice, will look out for a female of an honorable family, with whom I may hope for that happiness which you have assurred me is to be found in the undivided affec-tions of one only."

Mercutio felt a strong inclination to converse with his fair country-women : He communicated his de-sire to Kerim, who immediately gave orders to an Eunuch to conduct them to a private apartment, for that purpose : His order was instantly obeyed, and our hero flew on the wings of curiosity to meet them.

On being admitted, he approached them in a respect-ful manner, and, saluting them in their own language, requested them to banish their surprize ; informed them that his only motive for requesting the favor of the in-terview, was merely for the happiness of a few minutes converfation, and begged them to confider him as a perfon much interefted in their welfare : He immediately difcovered them to be the fame who had, more than all the reft, attracted the notice of himfelf and his friends, in the Harem.

They were aftonifhed at fuch a prelude, and were unable to form a conjecture of its leading object ; and for fome moments remained filent. Reflecting, however, on their fituation, they conceived his profeffions to be founded in artifice, and only calculated to throw them off their guard, and to inveigle them into a compliance with the defires of the Sophi, whom they confidered in no other light than as a libidinous tyrant, who wifhed to rifle them of that treafure which they were determined to preferve unpolluted, though at the hazard of their lives.

They returned his falute with a kind of diftant civility, and one of them informed him, that their virtue had been fufficiently tampered with without fuccefs, " which," faid fhe, " renders any further attempt to feduce us unneceffary ; therefore you may inform the tyrant who employed you to negociate this infamous bufinefs for him, that artifice will avail nothing ; that he need not expect to carry his point by ftratagem, and that force will be equally ineffectual, as we are determined not to furvive the lofs of our honour."

This rebuff delivered with an air of triumph, shook the confidence of Mercutio: however, by the fervency of his reply, he soon dispelled their doubts of his sincerity; their countenances brightened, and they listened to him with manifest pleasure.

They discoursed with freedom, and he convinced them of the sincerity of the Sophi's proffer of dismissing all his females; recited the particulars of his late conversation with him, and the resolution he had formed in consequence.

This information inspired the young ladies with new life; their eyes emitted new rays of satisfaction as he spoke, and they became almost frantic with gratitude. They embraced him alternately, styling him their deliverer, the preserver of their honour, and in the most emphatical terms, requested him to take them under his protection.

After listening with ecstasy to those tender effusions of gratitude, and having assured them of ample protection, he entreated them to inform him what accident had reduced them to their present situation.

The lady who had first addressed him, immediately began the following narration:

" Liverpool is the place of my nativity, where, at ten years of age, I experienced the loss of the best of mothers, my papa, disconsolate with his loss, resolved never to marry a second time, therefore sent to Bath for his sister, a maiden lady, to manage his domestic affairs, until I should arrive at years of maturity.

"My dear aunt was so extremely kind and tender, that my grief for the loss I had sustained, was in a short time almost obliterated. I was placed at a boarding school soon after my aunt arrived, where I was visited by my papa or my aunt once a fortnight, during my stay there. Having received such an education as was considered adequate to my sex and expectations, I returned to town, and my days rolled on happily for two years. At length, however, it pleased God to call my good aunt from this stage of care and anxiety; by which, much regretted circumstance, I became possessed of seven thousand pounds in the funds, and an annuity of three hundred per annum.

"A few months after my aunt's decease, my papa having occasion to transact some affairs in Holland, where his immediate presence was absolutely necessary; he left me to choose whether I would go and reside with a distant relation in Bristol, or accompany him in his voyage. I chose the latter without hesitation.

"In Amsterdam I formed an acquaintance with my companion, which soon ripened into a reciprocal friendship that has been gaining strength every day since.

"My papa, well acquainted with her brother, Mr. Wilcox, took lodgings in his house, where, after having fettled his affairs, to my unfpeakable grief, he was attacked by a malignant fever and kind of influenza, which in the courfe of fix weeks made me fatherlefs.

" In the early part of his illnefs, he made his will, appointing Mr. Wilcox his principal executor, and befides conftituting him his fpecial attorney, to recover feveral rents and fums of money not difpofed of by will.

" I remained with Mifs Wilcox and brother, who were in expectation of the arrival of their parents in Holland, when they intended to embark for England, whither I expected to accompany them; but an unfortunate circumftance took place, which deftroyed all our hopes, and was the caufe of our being reduced to the fhocking fituation in which you have found us; but as the latter part of the narrative more immediately relates to Mifs Wilcox, fhe will relate the particulars."

The other lady then began as follows:—

" Mifs Sydney has informed you, Sir, that our intimacy commenced in Amfterdam: Though this is the cafe, I am not a native of Holland. Florence is the place of my nativity, where I left my father and mother, befides a dearly beloved fifter with her hufband, an Englifhman, who is as dear to my parents as either of my brothers.

" My father is a native of Great-Britain, my mother of Florence, where he has been a refident more than

thirty years, and pursues the mercantile business, in
which few merchants have been more successful, as his
correspondence is fixed on the most extensive scale ; he
has several ships at sea—my eldest brother commands
one of them, in which he trades to the Levant ; and the
other has been my father's factor in Amsterdam, several
years : When he left Florence, I accompanied and remained with him until about six months ago.

"It is now about a year since, a young gentleman,
a native of Scotland, named Cameron, arrived in Amsterdam, and took lodgings in the house adjoining ours.

"As Mr. Cameron and my brother were engaged
in the same line of business, they soon contracted an
intimacy ; Mr. Cameron frequented our house on the
footing of my brother's bosom friend, and as such I
regarded him. He had not been more than two months
when he gave me to understand that I was not indifferent to him ; he took every convenient opportunity
to convince me of the sincerity of his professions ;
but for some time I paid very little attention to his discourse on this subject, as I felt no wish to alter my situation, and considered all the attention he paid me as
a thing of course ; therefore scarcely retained a syllable
of his discourse from one hour to another. However,
time, which changes the face and situation of all things,
made, in the course of six weeks, so material an alteration in my mind, that I sometimes was on the point
of doubting my own sanity ; but when I at length

took myself to task seriously, I did not find that unconcerned person, I had set myself down for. I found,
notwithstanding all the shifts and excuses made to myself, that I had admitted a dangerous inmate, one that
I dreaded would one day become a troublesome guest,
and lead me into difficulties, perhaps inextricable;
Alas! those forebodings are in a great measure realiz-
ed! May Heaven grant I have experienced all the
unhappiness which has resulted from my imprudence
in consenting to leave Amsterdam.

"Not to trouble you with a tedious recital of trivial
events, uninteresting to all perhaps but myself, I found
a strong prepossession in favor of Mr. Cameron, which
all my endeavors proved too languid to subdue : Mutual declarations of reciprocal attachment, was the result of our frequent interviews ; and it was at length
agreed, that Mr. Cameron should disclose the matter to
my brother, and urge him to consent to our union : In
this consultation and agreement, however, I lost sight of
my duty, in not taking into consideration the necessity
of my parents consent in a matter of such importance.

" My brother, as might have been expected, peremptorily rejected the proposal, as a very improper one,
and expressed his surprize that Mr. Cameron had made
it. " If my father was dead," said he, " it is not
improbable that I might consent ; at any rate the proposal would in that case, have stronger appearance of
propriety ; but as that is not the case, I must insist on
its being referred to him as to the only person in the

world who inherits the proper right to agree to, or reject it." " He expostulated with me in private, in the most serious, and at the same time, tender manner ; he exhorted me in the most forcible terms, to act cautiously in the matter, and conjured me by every tie of consanguinity, not to suffer my affections for Mr. Cameron to extinguish the remembrance of my duty ; nor to silence the admonitions of religion and reason.

" I was immediately sensible of my error—acknowledged the justice of his remarks, and proposed to avoid the company of Mr. Cameron until the arrival of my father."

" No, my dear sister," said he, " that is too great, sudden and perhaps dangerous a sacrifice to make. Mr. Cameron is a man of worth and probity, I have not the least doubt of his intentions and wishes being strictly honorable ; and it would afford me the highest satisfaction to see you happily united to so good a character : Perhaps I have given his feelings a momentary pang, by such a positive refusal ; but he is thoroughly sensible of the sincerity of my regard for him, therefore, one moment of cool reflection will remove it."

" Mr. Cameron was somewhat uneasy at first, but my brother took an opportunity of explaining the matter, and quickly convinced him of the necessity which obliged him to refuse his friend what he would much rather have granted.

" Their friendship suffered no diminution or relaxation in consequence of this circumstance, on the contrary, it was founded on a more broad and permanent basis than ever.

" Mr. Cameron, notwithstanding the repulse he had met with, resolved to make one effort more, in order to facilitate our union : In short, my brother, Mr. Cameron and myself, were fully perfuaded, that the confent of all my friends would be eafily and quickly obtained, and we all ardently wifhed for their arrival : A letter, however, from Florence arriving juft at that period, informed us, that owing to fome unexpected delays which had taken place, their embarkation would not be in lefs than twenty-five days. Mr. Cameron received this news like a fentence of death : He withdrew early in the evening, and I faw him no more for three days.

" He entered on the morning of the fourth, juft as we had fat down to breakfaft—and was as cheerful as I ever faw him. " Robert," faid he, " you have your affairs very near, if not entirely fettled, fuppofe you and I were to take a trip to Florence ? There is a fhip ready to fail in three days to Leghorn—it is a pleafant voyage, and will be an agreeable furprize to your friends to fee you once more on your native foil, before they leave it forever."

" Well," replied my brother, " it's an odd whim, and yet if it was not for an appointment I have made to

M VOL. II.

meet a gentleman in Leyden, on bufinefs of very great importance, exactly on this day week, I verily believe. I fhould accept your invitation."

" I am forry," faid Mr. Cameron, " that your appointment will deprive me of your company, for I will certainly go.   Come, ladies, as Mr. Wilcox is going to Leyden, you may as well accompany me, I am a ftranger to every one there, and have need of fome perfon to introduce me to Mr. and Mrs. Wilcox."

" I blufhed and felt embarraffed, I knew not why. Mifs Sydney and myfelf retired.

" At dinner, my brother informed me that he had actually given his confent for us to go to Florence, in cafe we would grant him ours.

" We looked at each other fome minutes without making any reply.   He proceeded—" Come, don't hefitate ; Mifs Sydney has never been in Italy—it will be an agreeable trip, and I dare engage you will not repent it : Mr. Cameron defired me to make this requeft ; for (faid he archly) Mifs Wilcox will not refufe me fo rational a favor——You have very little preparation to make, and I am fure he will employ every means to render your voyage agreeable."

" We at length confented, embarked and failed.

"For several days, we enjoyed the most perfect satisfaction ; a violent tempest however overtook us, which tossed us about three days and as many nights, during which time the Captain and mariners lost all hope ; which Mr. Cameron carefully concealed from us, and used every endeavor to keep us in good spirits, which, was a very difficult matter. But, by his appearing uniformly cheerful, we were deceived in respect to our danger, till one morning early, we were alarmed by the discharge of ordnance. The firing continued near half an hour, in which time Miss Sydney and myself were in the utmost distress ; the more so, as Mr. Cameron had not been below during the confusion.

"Conceive, if you can, Sir, what terror and astonishment pervaded our souls, when, after listening attentively for some time, and hearing men's voices, we perceived three men with turbans on their heads, and cimeters in their hands, enter the cabin !

"I uttered a loud shriek, and involuntarily called for Mr. Cameron. Miss Sydney instantly dropt into my arms motionless, which, I think prevented me from fainting—as my care for her in that moment, took place of every reflection on my own personal danger.

"The Turks, for such they were, ransacked the cabin of every thing of value that was portable—breaking up our trunks, the Captain's escrutoire, &c. &c.

"They difcourfed in a language we did not underftand, at the fame time pointing at Mifs Sydney and me
alternately, which left me no room to doubt of our fituation, or of our being the fubject of their difcourfe.

"Mifs Sydney had juft recovered fufficiently to be
fenfible of our horrid predicament, when I heard a voice
upon deck pronounce in Spanifh, which I underftood:
"Make hafte on board the galley—the prize is finking."

"We were inftantly compelled to leave the cabin,
and repair upon deck. Our people were already on
board the Pirate's veffel, and we were forced to follow,
with weeping eyes and palpitating hearts.

"The firft object that met my fight, was Mr. Cameron: Two of the Pirates were chaining him to the feat
where he was compelled to fit by the fide of one of our
feamen and row. The Captain was flain in the fkirmifh.

This fight deprived me of my fenfes for fome time;
my own diftrefs was totally forgot, and the thought of
his being in that fituation, rent my heart with anguifh.
It would be difficult to attempt a defcription of what I
fuffered on feeing him reduced to fuch extreme diftrefs,
more efpecially as I was fully fenfible that his love for
me alone had induced him to undertake the voyage. I
well knew he confidered himfelf as the caufe of my ruin,
which he no doubt concluded inevitable.

" On the other hand, I reproached myself as the origin of all the misfortunes, particularly those of Miss Sydney and myself. Mr. Cameron's hard fate would have been the same had I not consented to accompany him; but Miss Sydney and myself might have been happy in Amsterdam, had I been prudent enough to have refused.

" The Pirate conveyed us to Constantinople, where it was our good fortune to be transferred to a man, who brought us, without uttering one syllable, to this place; I call it good fortune, because we have been so happy as to meet with you, Sir, by whose generous interposition, I am in hopes of being restored to my friends and country once more.

" But where, oh where shall I seek for Mr. Cameron? Perhaps in this only interval of tranquillity we have experienced since our separation, he is subjected to all the injuries and insults of cruel Barbarians.

" The Sophi has employed all means but force to seduce us to his bed—his attempts have hitherto been fruitless. Miss Sydney has informed you of our resolution, never to survive the loss of honor, but vigorously to oppose every attempt to degrade us, and when death and ruin contend for dominion, cheerfully resign ourselves unpolluted, into the arms of the former, as the only sure alternative to escape the latter."

"Here she made a pause, and Mercutio, after polite-ly thanking her for her condescension, asked her the name of that brother whom she had mentioned as fol-lowing the sea. "His name is Nathaniel, Sir," said she.

"I have the honor of being intimately acquainted with your brother, as well as all the other friends you left in Florence," said he ; "and can assure you, he was in this city since you have been here."

This unexpected information astonished the ladies—they eagerly requested him to relate all he knew of Captain Wilcox and his friends. He fully gratified them, and added, if they were willing to submit them-selves to his care and protection, he would pledge his honor to see them restored to their friends. He in-formed them of his design of travelling through Russia, being determined to trust himself no more on the Me-diterranean.

To this proposal they mutually agreed, when he took his leave, with a promise of procuring their release-ment in a very short time.

Having rejoined his company in the garden, he com-municated the result of his conversation——It was agreed, to invest Isabella with the necessary powers to liberate the ladies. This commission she undertook with pleasure—happy in having it in her power to ad-minister relief to distressed innocence. She hasted joy-

fully to the fpot, and communicated her bufinefs to
them in a few words, and immediately conducted
them to the garden, where the Sophi and his friends
were bufy in difcourfe.

The two young ladies exprefled their gratitude to
their deliverers in the moft animated terms, and invoked
the favor of Heaven in behalf of Kerim ; who in the
cordial manner in which he faluted them, and the lively
fatisfaction vifible in his countenance, exhibited a convincing proof of the reality of that unadulteratrd pleafure which is the never failing refult of confcious rectitude : This reflection alone is fufficient to ftimulate us
to a punctual difcharge of every moral and focial duty,
not only as fuch, but as a pleafure.

In the viciffitudes of fortune, place and circumftances
which thefe young ladies experienced, the directing
hand of Providence may be readily traced. Had not
the Turk, who captured them, providentially met with
the Perfian to whom he fold them, it is more than probable, they would have been configned to the feraglio
of the Grand Senior, where they might have lingered
out their days in fuperlative mifery. Had they been
lefs virtuous, they would have met the advances of the
Perfian monarch, which would have proved an effectual bar to the performance of fuch extraordinary acts of
felf-denial, as Kerim had impofed on himfelf ; and had
not Providence directed Mercutio and his friends to
Ifpahan—or being there, had not happened to have

been the means of preserving the life of young Abbas, the whole concatenation must have been deranged, and the happy circumstance just described, could never have taken place.

Let the Atheist and Libertine—the one deny the existence of a God, and the other doubt the interpositi- on of Divine Providence ; yet, it is an undeniable truth, confirmed both by reason and revelation, and of which they will sooner or later be fatally convinced, that God is invariably the patron of virtue and punisher of vice ; and however the latter may, in the deluded opinion of its votaries, triumph over the former, its fancied superiority is but an empty shade—it is not capable of affording one single moment's felicity, and a melancholy catastrophe closes the scene ; while on the other hand, virtue, though apparently distressed, and often really embarrassed and beset with enemies, is productive of self-consolation ; and never fails to rise superior to every surrounding evil : In short, the result of an undeviating perseverance in the practice of virtue, is HAPPINESS.

Perhaps an enquiry into the fate of Mr. Wilcox and family, will not be unacceptable to the reader, in this stage of the narrative ; at all events I shall venture on it. Mr. Cameron, too, having been so intimately acquaint- ed with his son and daughter, deserves a share of our attention.

The former, we left at Constantinople, in the house provided by the Renegado who had captured them; the latter arrived there three days after. The very day after Isabella was taken from them, they were all taken out, in the habit of slaves, and exposed to public sale. They had stood more than two hours in this humiliating situation, when Mr. Wilcox noticed a man who seemed to view them with a solicitous eye; at length, he stept up to the old gentleman and craved his name. He had no sooner received the required information, than he turned short on his heel and approached the Renegado, who was at a small distance, and after some discourse, agreed with him for his whole capture; and taking him home to his own house, paid his demand and took his receipt.

The purchaser immediately hastened back to the spot where he had left the unhappy captives, and again addressing Mr. Wilcox, asked him if he would be willing to pass his bond to a person who would advance the money to ransom him and his company. He answered in the affirmative, and eagerly enquired his benefactor's name. "Suspend your curiosity for some time," said the stranger, "you shall be informed in due time: In the interim, you and your friends will accompany me to my house, it is not far off."

They were all filled with astonishment, but followed in silence. The stranger welcomed them to his house, and having drawn up a bond for the sum paid to the Renegado, laid it before him for signing.

On perusing the bond, Mr. Wilcox discovered his kind host to be a certain Aaron Levi, an eminent Jewish merchant, with whom he formerly had extensive dealings, and for whom he had once, not only negociated a difficult piece of business, but also advanced a very confiderable sum of money for him, which prevented the institution of a troublesome, if not ruinous lawsuit.

Levi's conduct on this occasion deserves our warmest approbation, and his manner of performing this disinterested action, enhanced the value of the favor in a ten fold degree.

The whole company expressed their sense of the obligation in the most ardent terms : Levi, however, seemed somewhat distressed with their acknowledgments, intreated them to desist, adding, that he had but discharged a debt long and lawfully due to Mr. Wilcox, and which he had long since wished for an opportunity of paying. Mr. Wilcox then executed the bond, and Levi continued : " You must unavoidably remain here some weeks. My house you see is large and commodious, and you are welcome to make your home here until you have an opportunity of sailing for Holland ; in the mean time, I insist on your accepting what money will be necessary to defray your expences, as I have enough of it, and you shall partake of it to the last ducat."

Without giving time for a reply, he defired the men to ftep afide with him a few minutes. He then conducted them to another apartment, where he furnifhed them with money, and gave them every neceffary inftruction with regard to clothes, and other neceffaries—left them full of grateful acknowledgments, requefting them to excufe him, as he had bufinefs of moment to tranfact that evening.

By the timely affiftance of Levi, thefe people, who but a few hours before, reduced to a fituation fimilar to the barbaroufly-treated Africans, having been expofed as objects of traffic, were now in the full enjoyment of perfonal freedom, together with the means of procuring the neceffaries and even luxuries of life.

In this defirable fituation we will leave them, while we take a view of that of Mr. Cameron, who was landed a prifoner in Conftantinople, the fecond day after the foregoing favorable change in their affairs took place.

George Wright happened to be ftanding at the very fpot where Mr. Cameron and feveral others were brought on fhore, and inftantly perceiving they were in the fame predicament in which he and his companions had fo lately been, furveyed them with the moft earneft attention. The Turk fpoke to them in broken Englifh, and George, anxious to hear the fubject of his difcourfe, advanced near enough to underftand that he was treating with a young man (Cameron) about his ranfom. The latter requefted permiffion to write to his friends in

England; and to remain unfold at Conftantinople, until the money fhould arrive; and affured the Turk he
fhould then have his full demand, which, by the bye was
no lefs than feven thoufand crowns : The Pirate appeared willing to agree, if any perfon could be found
who would enfure the conveyance of the letter ; but this
he very much doubted.

George, finding the bufinefs thus interefting, drew
near, and entered into difcourfe with the young man,
who was glad to hear the voice of an Englifhman there,
and at liberty; earneftly intreated his advice and affiftance; and told him the name of a nobleman to whom
he intended to apply for the ftipulated fum, as he was a
relation to whom he was well known, and on whom he
could confidently depend for relief.

George promifed him all poffible affiftance, and fug-
gefted, as the moft probable method to expedite the
bufinefs propofed, the propriety of an application to the
Britifh Conful, foliciting his affiftance in the matter.

Cameron approved the propofal, and George having
provided him the neceffary implements for writing,
he addreffed a pathetic letter to the Conful, in which
he gave a diftreffing defcription of his fituation ; and
fubjoined the ground of his expectations in England,
and laftly, requefted his direction and affiftance to
procure the much defired relief, without delay or difap-
pointment.

Having sealed this, he delivered it to George, who immediately set out, resolving to execute his commission with promptitude and punctuality.

The Consul, after perusing the letter, desired to see the bearer, who was instantly admitted. After some preliminary questions concerning the writer of the letter, he enquired how long he himself had been in Constantinople?

George satisfied him in all his interrogatories; but when he began to press him for an answer to the letter, he desired him to sit down and inform him in what part of the city he had left the author of the letter, adding, that he had a desire to see him, and would attend him to the spot, was he not prevented by the gout: At all events (said he) I will dispatch a servant with a message to his owner, which will probably procure his liberty for some time at least.

George proposed carrying the message himself, which the Consul did not oppose; but immediately writing a small note, delivered it to him, when he set out, and in a short time put it into the hands of the Renegado, who perused the billet, and turning to a Moorish boy, whispered something in his ear, who instantly disappeared. The Pirate then entered a house near the water-side, followed by George and Mr. Cameron, where they had not remained long, before the boy returned with a bundle, which his master ordered him to deliver to Mr. Cameron. It contained the best suit of his wearing apparel. The Pirate also returned him his gold watch, and purse containing about thirty-five guineas. Mr. Cameron withdrew to another apartment, and having changed his habit, was at liberty to attend George to the Consul's house.

The Consul gave them a cordial reception—his condescension appeared remarkable to them both, as they were not able to conjecture the cause; the sequel, however, will solve this apparent paradox:

Mr. Cameron's mother, possessed of beauty, birth and fortune, to which may be added, wit, virtue and discretion, took the liberty at the age of twenty years, to bestow her heart and hand to the father of Mr. Cameron, a gentleman who never disgraced his name, country or religion, and was highly deserving the character he bore, which was that of a merchant of the most extensive property, and inflexible integrity: He was thirty years of age at the time of his marriage, which was contracted by and with the consent of her mother, a widow lady, and his friends; but in diametrical opposition to that of her two brothers, who, proud of their high hereditary birth, titles and pedigree, considered an alliance with a merchant, an indelible blemish to their race; and resolved, in consequence, never to forgive the CRIME she had committed against their name and dignity. The uprightness of Mr. Cameron's dealings, however, soon established his reputation among

all ranks, on an immoveable bafis. His brothers-in-
law, notwithstanding the falfe principles of honor they
had imbibed by education, were by no means void of
difcernment or generofity; therefore, as years ripened
their judgment, their prejudices vanifhed, and they
were conftrained to do juftice to the merits of a relation
who was a real honor to their family, by a generous
and cordial reconciliation : The two families were by
this means united in the ftricteft bonds of friendfhip.
About this time the birth of a beautiful boy cemented
the union with ftill greater ftrength ; for as he grew up,
he became the particular favorite of his two uncles, one
of whom infifted on being at the fole expence of his
education, which may be fuppofed was liberal.

It was to this generous uncle, that Mr. Cameron,
(who was the identical fon and favorite beforementioned) intended to write for the fum demanded for his
ranfom ; (his father died before he vifited Holland) and
the Conful happily proved to be his other uncle.

As if actuated by one foul, the Conful and his happy
nephew rofe at one inftant, and advancing eagerly, exchanged the warmeft embraces. " My dear nephew,"
faid the former, " though I fincerely fympathize in
your misfortunes ; yet, as I have it in my power to
procure your freedom immediately, and have the pleafure of feeing you in perfect health, I feel a fuperior
degree of fatisfaction, in this providential opportunity
of teftifying at once my tendereft regard to my fifter, by

manifesting the most disinterested esteem for her son, and
the purest fraternal regard to my beloved brother, to
whom I know you are most dear."

Mr. Cameron was overwhelmed with joy, gratitude
and amazement, and after giving vent to the enthusi-
astic effusions of his heart, gently upbraided George, for
not apprizing him of the scene he was to expect.

" The gentleman," said his uncle, interrupting him,
" knew no more than yourself our consanguinity at that
time.   When I saw in your letter your wish to write
to my brother, and your expectation of relief from him,
I passed over the rest, and seeing the subscription, I was
too impatient to read any more, and immediately resolved to effect your deliverance before I saw you.
This gentleman has been but very lately redeemed, he
has informed me, from the Turks, together with several
friends and relatives, who are now in this city, waiting
for an opportunity of returning to Great-Britain."

Mr. Cameron now returned the most grateful acknowledgments to George, for his kind conduct, and
the Consul added a most cordial invitation to him and
all his friends, to dine with him the ensuing day : He
promised to deliver the message, and to attend himself.

Being now alone with his nephew, the Consul began
to enquire the cause of his voyage, intended place of
destination, and manner of being captured. To all of

which he answered ingenuously, and concluded with a most passionate lamentation for the loss of Miss Wilcox and her companion, Miss Sydney.

'The Consul perceived, by comparing George's relation with that of his nephew, that the young lady, the loss of whom was so much deplored by the latter, must undoubtedly be the sister-in-law to the former. He communicated this suspicion to Mr. Cameron—observing, that her father was a native of England, but had been many years a resident in Florence—that he had a son in Amsterdam—and, that he had retired from business, and was returning to his native country, to spend the remainder of his days in the midst of his children, when he fell into the hands of the Infidels.

" My dear Sir," answered Mr. Cameron, " your suspicions I plainly see are but too well founded—a thousand circumstances croud my mind at once, and all combine to prove it. How shall I meet her parents to-morrow? Whence collect fortitude enough to support a painful interview with persons whom I have so deeply injured?—Her consent, which was in a manner extorted, to accompany me to Florence, will avail nothing with parents robbed of such a treasure ; to urge it, would be little short of insult."

'The Consul agreed with his kinsman in part ; but told him he had no doubt of bringing about a reconciliation. He remarked, that the recovery of the ladies was not altogether impossible, though if in the Seraglio, extremely difficult—but thought it probable that some information might be drawn from the Pirate, which might lead to a discovery.

An intelligent domestic was immediately dispatched, and soon returned, accompanied by the Pirate, who being interrogated by the Consul, informed, that he had disposed of them to a Persian, who talked of setting out for Ispahan immediately. The Consul promised to reward him liberally, if he would immediately use every endeavor to discover the Persian, if not yet gone ; and if he was, to gain every possible information of his route.

It was late in the evening when he returned, and all the intelligence he had been able to obtain was, that his name was Aspendi, a native of Ispahan, and had sat out immediatly after the purchase.

Mr. Cameron was no sooner informed of the course he had taken, than he formed the resolution to follow, and if possible to overtake and obtain the release of the ladies, or perish in the enterprize. He acquainted his uncle with this design : Who, although he did not altogether approve of the plan, did not attempt to dissuade him from it : On the contrary, he told him if he persisted in the undertaking, he should be at no loss for any thing necessary to the attainment of the object of his pursuit.

In order to save Mr. Cameron the confusion of being present, his uncle proposed his retiring to any adjoining chamber, where he might remain and hear all that passed between Mr. Wilcox and the company, without the mortification of being observed to betray, what he termed symptoms of guilt, until notice was given him to make his appearrnce.———These preliminaries being settled, they retired to rest.

At the appointed time, Mr. Wilcox, attended by all his friends, waited on the Consul, who received them with politenefs and freedom ; the ladies in particular, he treated with uncommon attention.

As the principal aim of the Consul in this conference, was to lay the foundation of a reconciliation between his relation and Mr. Wilcox and family, he soon found means to give the conversation a turn from general subjects, to that of the accident, which, as he expressed it, had procuredhim the honor of a visit from so respectable a company of Christians, in the capital of the Turkish empire.

This naturally introduced an account of Mr. Wilcox's former line of business, his connections in England, &c. The Consul generously sympathized in their misfortunes ; at the same time, he assured them of his kind offices, and of a safe passport through the Streights. They testified their acknowledgments in terms of undissembled gratitude. His generosity rested not here—He had sent for Mr. Levi, whose name was just then an-

nounced by a domestic, and being introduced, was in-
vited to sit down. "I have heard a most respectable
account of you, Mr. Levi, (said the Consul) which
entitles you greatly to my esteem: A good man I re-
vere, be his name, country or religion what they may.
I am further informed, that you have a bond of this
gentleman's—will you be pleased to let me see it?"——
He immediately produced the bond, which the Consul
perused, and returned it, saying, You are a worthy man,
Mr. Levi—you will give up this paper to Mr. Wilcox,
and I will advance you the whole sum to-morrow, as
well as all other demands you may have against him.
Perceiving Mr. Wilcox about to make some acknowledgments, he prevented him by a motion of the hand.

Levi surrendered the bond with pleasure, saying,
My very good friend, here is your bond, and I wish it
was in my power to replace all the Pirates have deprived
you of—you should then see with what cheerfulness
I would serve you.

Nothing could exceed the gratitude and admiration
of those people: Every remembrance of their late misfortunes were absorbed in the contemplation of the un-
exampled instances of magnanimity exercised towards
them by the Consul and Mr. Levi: The latter apolo-
gizing for the shortness of his stay, on the score of ur-
gent business, was excused, on condition of renewing
his visit the ensuing day——He then withdrew.
The Consul having now brought matters in a suitable

train, called their attention to an important piece of information, in which, he assured them, they were deeply interested.

Accordingly, after some observations, calculated to pave the way to a reconciliation between his kinsman and Mr. Wilcox, he informed them of every circumstance relative to Miss Wilcox and Mr. Cameron, as before related ; and concluded with an earnest request, that his nephew might obtain pardon of the whole family, as his error originated in the noblest of principles, and as he had the consent of their son as well as the young lady herself :—He further assured them of the sincere contrition, and of his determination to pursue the Persian who had the ladies in custody, and bring them back at the risk of his life.

His pardon was pronounced with much sincerity ; but to suppress the rising sigh and gushing tear, was an effort to which the fortitude of Mrs. Wilcox was inadequate—nor were the rest of the company unconcerned. George's wife and Terentia withdrew to vent their grief in private ; in short, a gloomy sadness diffused itself over the whole, when the preconcerted notice being given, Mr. Cameron made his appearance. He instantly advanced, and on his knees implored forgiveness of Mr. and Mrs. Wilcox, in such an affecting manner, that they both pronounced his pardon in loud, inarticulate sobs : The whole company caught the contagion, and not an eye in the room but shed the tear of sympa-

-thy—honorable badge of noble sentiment! of refined humanity!

Mr. Cameron began the next day to make preparations for his expedition, and was ready to sail in four days, a vessel having been provided through the interest of his uncle, for that particular service, which was to remain at Trapesond fifteen days for his return.

He had a quick and pleasant passage to Trapesond, where he was attacked with a slight intermittent, which confined him eight days to his bed. A very favorable circumstance, however, took place, which in all human probability, was a principal mean of saving his life, for his lodging was very indifferent, and medical aid was not to be obtained.

Captain Wilcox and Mr. Fitzgerald parted in Ardevil; the latter shaped his course through Tefflis to Aftracan, and the former proceeded to Trapesond, in order to take shipping for Constantinople. Captain Wilcox fortunately took his quarters at the identical house where Mr. Cameron was lying sick. As all the Eastern languages, by his long intercourse with the natives, had become as habitual to him as his own, he discoursed with ease in any of them. His first enquiry after his arrival, was for a vessel bound to Constantinople. He was informed, there was but one, and that was to remain some time, to wait for a gentleman who was lying there sick.

This information naturally led to an enquiry of where he came from? whither he was bound? and what his complaint was? To the first of these questions only, he received a satisfactory answer, and being informed he was not a Mussulman, expressed a desire to see him. He was accordingly conducted to his apartment, where he found him in a very languid state: His good constitution had conquered the malady, and all that was then necessary, was some powerful restoratives to re-establish him in his usual vigour.

The Captain, at a very great expence and much entreaty, procured some wine—fowls were plenty, and he kindly undertook the office of purveyor, cook and nurse; and by his kind attention, with the assistance of heaven, Mr. Cameron was in a few days able to walk out with him. It was not till then, that Captain Wilcox attempted to hold any conversation with his patient, except such as immediately related to his health.

One fine day, the Captain proposed going on board the vessel, which lay at anchor about a quarter of a mile from the shore. Cameron assented, and they immediately set out. In the course of this day's conversation, they became mutually known to each other. Mr. Cameron disclosed circumstantially, every thing relative to his friends in Constantinople—his own adventures and misfortunes—his business in Persia, and his resolution not to return without the ladies.

The Captain generously embraced him. "Came‑
ron," said he, "you are possessed of a noble soul, and
I should consider myself worse than an infidel, if I was
capable of wounding your feelings by withholding the
hand of friendship. My sister I love most dearly—I
well know if she is not recovered soon, the remem‑
brance of her loss will plant a dagger in the heart of my
mother; but as I am convinced your intentions with
regard to her, were strictly honorable, I assure you of
my forgiveness and friendship; and if she is irrecovera‑
bly gone, we must endeavor to sustain the shock with
firmness, and console ourselves with the reflection that
our virtuous intentions far exceeded our foresight. But
since fortune has brought us together, and you give me
such pleasing assurances of the prosperous situation of
our friends in Constantinople, I am determined to ac‑
company you to Ispahan; as it is but very lately I left
that city, I expect to find some friends who will gladly
assist us in our research."

Mr. Cameron was quite overwhelmed with the con‑
tinued kindness and generosity; and his offer of accom‑
panying, afforded him the most genuine satisfaction.
His health being firmly established, they set out for Ar‑
devil, three hundred and thirty-three miles from Ispahan
nearly the centre between the places of departure and
destination.

Just before their departure, Captain Wilcox learn
of the host, that according to his description, the ob‑
jects of their pursuit had lodged there, on their way to

Ardevil, and that the ladies seemed in great distress—having never laid down, but walked backwards and forwards the whole night, crying and sobbing most bitterly.

In consequence of this intelligence, they resolved to lose no time; and therefore pressed forward with more than ordinary speed. One fine evening, the moon rising in her full splendor, and the cooling zephyrs having dissipated the sultry beams of the day, afforded them such delightful sensations, that they determined to ride all night.

The point of time we are now speaking of, was the very day after that on which Kerim received the news of the revolt. Just as the day began to dawn, they were surrounded by a detachment of cavalry, and having no means for defence or flight, they were conducted to Casbin, and there closely confined as spies, until that sanguinary scene was past. Captain Wilcox, however, at last, with the never-failing influence of a sum of money, prevailed on his keeper to make application to the principal magistrate to have them brought to trial, if there was any accusation against them; and if not, to be set at liberty, and be permitted to proceed on their journey. The result of this application was, their being conducted under a strong guard to Ispahan, to be examined by the Sophi, as the Magistrates of Casbin concurred in the opinion of their being Russians in disguise, in the interest of the rebel chief; but, admitting that to be the case, they knew not what to do with them. Though this circumstance was by no means a pleasing one, yet, conscious of their innocence, they were not without hopes of a discharge, if justice could be obtained.——We will leave them on their journey, and look after Mercutio and his companions.

The day preceding that fixed on for their departure Kerim devoted entirely to conversation with his friends; and though it was the last, in all human probability, they would ever meet together, it was spent in the usual unrestrained manner; and whatever might be thought, not a single expression escaped one of the company, which had the smallest tendency to remind them of their approaching separation, until late at night. Kerim in the most serious manner, enjoined Mercutio to write from every stage of their journey, and pointed out a very eligible plan of correspondence from England by the way of Russia.

He informed them, that they would be at no trouble about their passage to Astracan, as there was a vessel ready to receive and carry them as far up the Walgo river as they thought proper to sail.

"And now, my inestimable friends," said he, " I feel myself unable to support the painful emotions which I am very sensible a separation will inevitably excite; therefore, may the Supreme Disposer of all events confer on you all, every thing requisite to constitute your temporal and eternal happiness !"——As he pronouned these last wor ds. he arose ..n his sopha, and laying his hand ... ... said———— " Kerim bids you adieu" ... ... vate door opened, and he instantly disappea... Mercutio arose to intercept him—but he was gone, and the door shut with a spring.

Egyptian darkness eclipsing the meridian sun, could not have had a more instantaneous, powerful effect on their corporeal as well as mental faculties, than had this sudden exit of the Sophi ! An irresistable stupor diffused itself over the whole company : They for some moments sat silent and motionless as so many statues !

Abbas, first resuming the conversation, informed them, that his father had apprized him of his intention in the morning, assigning the same reason he had hinted to them a few minutes past ; and added, that he had obtained his permission to accompany them to the Caspian sea, " I have, (said he) repeatedly pressed my father for leave to accompany you to England ; but his answer was uniformly this, that the loss of you would most sensibly afflict him—and if I should go, there would remain no manner of consolation for him—his palace would become a prison, and his gardens deserts : In short, every surrounding object would awaken the painful reflection of pleasures, which were never to return, which he was sure would soon put a period to his existence. " For these reasons, my son," he would add, " your request cannot at present be granted—but it is possible, that time may in some measure reconcile me to my fate—when I shall hea   their being safely settled in their native country—and when   m sure of your having such a company of honorable frien?s to receive and welcome you in Europe, I will not withhold my consent : In the mean time, my Abbaſs, be content. To tell you how ardently I love you—how near your intereſt and your pleaſures concern me, would be a waſte of time and language. I ſhall take my final leave of them this night ſuddenly : They may (but they know me well) ſuppoſe my behavior on the occaſion rather abrupt,—and my reaſon for giving you theſe hints, is in order that you may explain and place the matter in ſuch a point of view as may remove every doubt of the continuance of that unſhaken regard which I had and do ſtill retain for them."

The night being far advanced, they retired to reſt for the laſt time under the roof of the more than hoſpitable monarch of Perſſia—while Abbaſs went to iſſue the neceſſary and ſpecial orders for the early attendance of the guards, &c.

Before the Oriental beams had gladdened their horizon, Mercutio and his friends aroſe ; but found the vigilant, and no leſs affectionate Abbaſs at the gate. A troop of one hundred horſe waited to eſcort them, while two camels bent beneath the weight of the Sophi's bounty.

Every thing in such a state of forwardness, they were ready by the time the sun appeared above the horizon, to set out. Abbafs, in all the magnificence of an Eastern Prince, was the foremost to assist Isabella in mounting ; while tears of the most sincere regard bedewed the threshold of the palace as they issued forth.

The weather being uncommonly fine, the journey to the sea side was remarkably pleasant ; and no disagreeble incident intervened, to interrupt their speed or damp their cheerfulness. Arriving at the point of embarkation, they found another instance of Kerim's peculiar regard displayed : A new galley, on the most beautiful construction, built for that particular service, most gorgeously furnished and adorned, lay at anchor in a small cove or inlet, where they could embark with the greatest ease and convenience.

The burthens were by the command of Abbafs taken off the camels and conveyed on board the galley. They then embarked, but it was agreed to write one last adieu, and dispatch it to Kerim, before the anchor was weighed : Accordingly, Mercutio set down and penned the following, which was translated by Abbafs into Arabic :—

" MOST VIRTUOUS PRINCE,

" Long, very long, we have been in a great measure exiled from our native country and dearest connections ; yet, on leaving the Persian confines, we find it impossi-

ble to reftrain the tributary tear of gratitude due to the
benevolent Kerim, and equally impoffible to remain infenfible to the pang of feparation—a pang which the
envious, the felfifh and the malevolent are unfufce tible.
What then? Can the noble, the generous Kerim, fuppofe we prefer any nation in the univerfe to that which
gave us breath? Can he conceive that the tear of regret,
which we now mingle with the briny billows of the
Cafpian, is fhed for the lofs of thofe diftinguifhed attentions with which we have uniformly been, and ftill are
honored, ever fince our arrival in the Perfian dominions?
No, Kerim, it proceeds from a more exalted, a more
noble fource. Thofe emotions which now agitate our
bofoms, have their origin in the moft fincere friendfhip;
and when we caft the laft retrofpective glance o'er the
cloud-topped Tauris, we fhall unite our lamentations,
not for leaving Perfia, but its Monarch—the beft of
Men—the beft of Princes! To be deprived of fociety
fuch as this, affords us fufficient caufe of regret: This
alone is capable of giving us, at this time, any concern.

" Accept, amiable Prince, this departing teftimony
of our lafting efteem! Preferve it as an acknowledgment of the many and exceedingly great favors with
which we are, even now loaded, by the unbounded
liberality of Kerim.

" We unite our moft ardent prayers for your long and
happy reign. May unanimity prefide in, and wifdom
direct your councils—loyalty pervade the hearts of all

your subjects, and faction be eternally banished from your dominions. Fraught with these sentiments, we bid you a friendly adieu.

" P. S. Abbafs fails with us to Aftracan—no farther."

The foregoing was figned by them all ; and it was not till that moment that Abbafs conceived the idea of accompanying them to Aftracan, which afforded them much fatisfaction ; and having fealed and difpatched the letter, Abbafs took a few guards on board, and gave orders for the reft to remain on the fpot until his return, the anchor was immediately weighed, and the fails expanded to a profperous breeze : The elaftic oars quickly encreafed the velocity of the galley, fo that they performed the voyage in a fhort time.

They lay before Aftracan forty-eight hours, in which time, Abbafs engaged a light veffel to tranfport him back. His vivacity, however, forfook him, as the time of feparation approached, and a vifible alteration took place in the appearance of the whole company. How-ever, part they muft, and all defcription would fall in-finitely fhort of its intended purpofe, in attempting the fcene that took place on the occafion—fuffice it to fay, they parted with much regret on both fides, and failed in different directions in the fame inftant.———And now leaving them on their paffage, we will enquire into the fate of Captain Wilcox and Mr. Cameron.

They were on their examination at the very inſtant in which Abbaſs arrived. Captain Wilcox's narration procured them not only an honorable releaſe, but the kinleſt treatment. Nothing could exceed the joy of Mr. Cameron and his fellow traveller, when the Sophi informed them of the ſafety and unblemiſhed virtue of the two ladies. They reſolved to exert all their diligence to overtake Mercutio and his friends; and, if poſſible, perſuade them to repair with them to Conſtantinople, and there embark for England, in company with Mr. Wilcox and the reſt of his friends. They communicated their intention to the Sophi, who perſuaded them from the attempt, by aſſuring them of the little probability of their being overtaken, as he expected they were then at Saratow; and gave it as his opinion, that they had better bend their courſe towards Trapeſond, and from thence, with all poſſible ſpeed to Conſtantinople; adding, that by this means, the two parties would very probably make Holland at the ſame time.

Being convinced of the propriety of purſuing this advice, and the Sophi having read the letter from Mercutio, reſolved to write an anſwer, and commit it to the care of Captain Wilcox. Abbaſs alſo, proud of ſuch an opportunity, determined to follow the example of his father, in tranſmitting to his beloved tutor and friends, a written teſtimony of his eſteem. This done, the Sophi ordered two excellent horſes to be completely equipped, inſtead of their own, which were taken from them at Casbin ; and at parting, forced each of them, notwithstanding reiterated refusals, to accept a large sum of money, which, he jocosely said, was but justly due for false imprisonment.

They reached Constantinople without any interruption, and found their friends in high health—their spirits were greatly exhilerated on seeing Captain Wilcox once more ; and when they heard of the safety of the young ladies, their joy was complete.

There being nothing now to detain them in Constantinople, but the want of a vessel to transport them, they began to arrange matters for their departure. Mr. Cameron waited on his uncle as soon as he arrived, and gave a full relation of his good fortune ; and as he had not the least cause to doubt of obtaining the approbation of all Mr. Wilcox's family to his marriage with the object of his wishes, he informed his uncle of his resolution to accompany them to Holland, and from thence to England.

The Consul being determined to secure his kinsman's happiness, if possible, before they departed, sent a very polite invitation to Mr. and Mrs. Wilcox, together with all their friends, requesting their company the next day. They waited on him accordingly, when he took the opportunity of heartily congratulating Mr. Wilcox and lady on the recovery of their son and daughter, in doing which, he easily discovered, that Mr. Cameron

stood on firm ground. He therefore hinted the subject
to Mr. Wilcox apart, who assured him, he knew of no
obstacle between Mr. Cameron and his daughter, provided she had not changed her mind.

This benevolent man then informed them, that he had
not been altogether indifferent to their interests; but
had taken such effectual measures to serve them, that
he had actually recovered the ship in which they sailed
from Leghorn, although she had been transferred four
different times, and was then at Lemnos. He assured
them she would certainly arrive in a few days, together
with eight hands, whom he hand ransomed, that were
taken with Mr. Cameron, and whom he had sent under
an experienced pilot to navigate the ship: "With
these," he added, "together with a few that may be
picked up here, will probably be deemed sufficient,
under the command of Captain Wilcox, to navigate
her safely to England."

The grateful acknowledgments of these much obliged
people, could no longer be suppressed: The favors
they had received, were of too great magnitude only to
admit of a mere complimentary return;—the sincere
effusions of sensibility gushed forth like a torrent from
every heart—and tears of gratitude bedewed every
cheek. The consciousness of having contributed to
the happiness of such a company, who but a few weeks
before were condemned to the most ignominious and
cruel bondage, must doubtless have afforded the Consul

a heart-felt pleasue ; which, however, was considerably heightened by its having also been a secondary
mean of endearing Mr. Cameron still more to the only
family in the world to which he most ardently wished
to be united.

The expected ship at length arrived, and Captain
Wilcox having engaged six additional hands, went on
board to put all things in sailing order. This being
completed, the Consul furnished him with a Mediterranean pass, and then accompanied all hands on board.
Here he presented his nephew with bills on London
for fifteen thousand pounds, which, he said, were for his
nuptial expences : Then, taking an affectionate fare-
well of them all, and wishing them a good voyage,
returned on shore, while our voyagers invoked the blessings of heaven for their beloved, benevolent benefactor.

As no material occurrence happened to interrupt
their voyage or tranquillity, we will leave them without
the Streights of Gibraltar, and follow our hero through
the Russian territories, on his way to his native country.

He chose that route, not as the nearest, or easiest ;
but as the safest. He had been so often foiled in attempting to regain his native land, and the most of his
disasters happening in the Mediterranean, he was resolved never to trust himself within the Streights again.
They arrived at Moscow without any accident. The
ladies bore the fatigue admirably ; however, as the

caravan was not to fet out for Peterfburgh, in lefs than
ten days, they took up their abo. e in a very commodious Inn, where every neceffary for themfelves and their
cattle was to be ha in abundance, determining to re-
gale themfelves with a fight of whatever appeared
worthy of obfervation in that famous city.

Their hoft, though in the habit of Mufcovy, and
though he wore a beard of great length, appeared to
our travellers to carry about him certain peculiarities of behavior, which inclined them to believe, that
he was a native of Great-Britain, or that he certainly
muft have refided among the Englifh fome years: One
particular circumftance which ftrengthened their fuf-
picion was, that although he fpoke the Ruffian dialect
alone, yet he underftood Englifh perfectly—furnifhed
them with every thing they demanded, and appeared
very affiduous, though much on the referve. They
perceived but two females about the houfe; one, a
middle aged Dutch woman, who fpoke tolerable Englifh, and the other a young Ruffian girl: They were,
however, both fervants, therefore, it was concluded
that their hoft was a widower. Mercutio propofed
inviting him to fup with them one night, which was
agreed to, as they all poffeffed a curiofity to know
fomething of his real character, for they did not believe him to be a Ruffian.

He accepted the invitation. The ladies retired foon
after fupper, and the glafs circulated pretty freely.

They had hitherto never been able to procure an answer
to any question but through the medium of his Dutch
house-keeper, or by an assenting nod. Mercutio, however, finding his usual gravity considerably relaxed,
addressing him in French, asked him whether he was
really what he pretended to be, a Russian. His answer,
in a very good style of French, was a negative; and
after various turns of conversation, and a few additional
bumpers of claret, he freely avowed himself an Englishh-
man. On being asked the reason of his making choice
of such a place and employment, secluded from the
company of every person who could discourse with him
in his own language; and contrary to the inclinations
of mankind in general, to conform to the language,
customs, and even dress of a foreign nation, in every
respect totally different from his own? He hinted that
every nation in the world, had it its own peculiarities,
pleasures and inconveniencies: That he was as completely reconciled to those of Russia, as if he was a native; that although the rough and disagreeable countenances of the Russians disgusted him on his first arrival,
he had discovered, while serving in their army, many
valuable characters; and that the rough outside of the
Russians, in general, as well obscured many shining
qualities and good hearts, as the insinuating smiles and
polished address of some other nations, concealed the
avaricious hypocrite and the parasitical pander.

He at length related in English the whole of his adventures. He informed them that he was the son of a

British peer, and had been engaged in an affair of gallantry with a married lady ; that he had been detected in the fact by her husband, and in a rencontre with him on the spot, received a wound which nearly terminated his life ; and that his antagonist immediately left the kingdom and was never heard of afterwards. In short, they found in their Muscovite host, the son of the Earl of Oxford, whom Charles left in his wife's bed-chamber, weltering in his gore, apparently in the agonies of death.

As he concealed no part of the story, his ignorance of the persons to whom he was relating it, was sufficiently obvious, they therefore took care not to let the discourse slack until they learnt the issue of that affair.

He informed them, that his wound was pronounced mortal at the first dressing ; his surgeon declaring it very dangerous to attempt moving him, he was therefore compelled to remain in the very chamber to reflect on the disagreeable consequences of an approaching eternity.

" The third day after " (continued the host) " I was visited by her father-in-law, whose presence covered me with confusion, for I still considered myself as a dead man, the surgeon having given me no encouragement to even hope to recover ; I therefore candidly confessed the whole intrigue, and begged his forgiveness."

" Go, go," said he, " yet, unworthy as you are, I

will not reproach you in your present situation: But remember, your soul hangs over a dreadful abyss; your manifold crimes are crushing you downward, and oh! consider the dreadful consequences of leaving this world with such a weight of guilt unrepented of. The attempt to seduce an unmarried woman is ungenerous, base and cowardly, but not so fatal in its consequences, if it succeeds, as if she is a wife: In the first case, the reputation, peace of mind, and indeed all that could render life desirable to the unhappy victim, is destroyed; and all the hopes of her parents blasted:—In the second, the stigma which will inevitably be fixed on her innocent offspring, if she has children, and the dishonor of her injured husband, the anguish of whose mind, and just spirit of resentment, may perhaps tempt him rashly to take the life of his betrayer, or in the contest lose his own, and perhaps both, adds a three-fold degree of horror to the crime." Saying these words, he left the room, and meeting his daughter-in-law at the head of the stairs, ordered her to prepare to leave a house on which she had fixed the first stain of adultery, and of blood, the consequence of that adultery. He was deaf to her prayers and entreaties for forgiveness; he spurned her from him, and left the house instantly.

"Notwithstanding the prediction of the surgeon, I was soon out of danger. An application was made at Doctors Commons, and a divorce obtained by the time I was fit to be removed, so we both left the house together. As soon as I was thoroughly recovered, I married her, and my father being fully informed of the whole affair, disinherited me, and would neither see or receive a letter from me afterwards.

"In this dilemma I was at a loss what course to take, and at length resolved to endeavor to procure a commission in the army just then going to America; but was prevailed upon by my wife to abandon the design. She observed, that since her relations had refused all manner of connection and correspondence with her, and being deprived of every friend in the world except myself, she could not think of depending upon the uncertain fate of war for support.

"Being still able to command about twelve hundred pounds, and with that I determined to fix my residence in Petersburgh, until an opportunity might offer of making application to the Empress for a genteel post in the Russian service.

"I had not been long in that capital before I found means of access to the Princess. She presented me an honorable commission, which I had only borne ten days, when I received orders to attend the new Khan of the Crimea to his government. He was a young Prince of great valor, whom the Empress had newly appointed to the government of that part of her dominions. As my orders were to remain there some months, my wife accompanied me.

" The young Prince was scarcely settled in his government, when a vast body of insurgents, headed by his two brothers, invaded his dominions. He courageously gave them battle, and was supported with unparalelled bravery; yet, he had the mortification to see his army hewn to pieces before his eyes, and himself with a few select friends, obliged to abandon the capital to the rapine and plunder of the invaders. I saw my wife killed with a lance, and was not able to afford her any relief or consolation, being engaged with a force greatly superior to my own, in rescuing the young Prince from a party of Rebels, by whom he had been surrounded and taken.

" We conducted the young Prince by a circuitous route, to Petersburgh, when I immediately resigned my commission and retired to this place, which I intend to leave next year, and remove to South-Carolina, in North America, with what I have accumulated, where I expect to end my days, for I am resolved never to return to England."

As he did not yet appear to have the least knowledge of either Augustus or Charles, both of whom the reader will recollect, he he had seen in England, they resolved to leave him in ignorance. Accordingly, the next day they set forward for Petersburgh, along that famous road which Peter the Great caused to be opened through the wilderness, from Petersburgh to Moscow, a distance of near five hundred miles, and as straight as a line.

As they stopped to refresh at a small town, within two
days journey of Petersburgh, they were met by a company of soldiers on their march.   It was evening, and
both parties remained in town, till the next day.   It
happened that the Russian officers quartered at the same
inn where our travellers put up.   Our hero was much
surprized at hearing the commanding officer of the detachment, giving some private directions to a subaltern,
in a very familiar style, and in good English.   He took
an opportunity, when he perceived him at leisure, to
ask him where the troops under his command were
destined ?

He replied to Moscow, on a secret and important
expedition.   Though this answer was given with the
most polite affability, effectually prevented further enquiry ; however they discoursed on different subjects,
and soon became highly delighted with each other's
company.   In the mean time, Charles and Augustus
were taking a view of the Russian soldiery, and was
immediately struck with the appearance of the Lieute-
nant, who in the same instant recollected and flew to
embrace them.

This officer was no other than Mr. Fitzgerald. They
were overjoyed to meet him in such an honorable situation, and began to enquire how he had been thus successful in so short a time.   After the most eager and
friendly enquiries for our hero and Mr. Wilcox, he informed them, that his commander was his own brother.

"But come," said he, "I must introduce you to him —he already holds you in high estimation from my account, and will be very happy to see you."

He immediately conducted them to the room where our hero was seated in discourse with his brother. "Here, brother," said he, "are the gentlemen of whom you have so often heard me speak, that I left in Ispahan." Reciprocal salutations of the warmest friendship were exchanged, and Mercutio proposed spending the evening together, which being assented to, the two Fitzgeralds were introduced to the ladies. The evening was spent in the most convivial manner; in the course of which our hero and his companions collected full information on the subject of the secret expedition to Moscow.

The Empress had received private and certain intelligence of a combination then forming, between a young restless Prince of the Don Cossacs, and the heads of the Calmuc, Circassian and Georgian Tribes, to seize on Moscow, and proclaim the young Cossac Emperor. They had emissaries in all parts of Moscow, who were paving the way to a general revolt, among whom, was their late quondam host. It was to secure those principal mal-contents, and to convey them to Petersburgh, that Colonel Fitzgerald was leading his detachment : A formidable body of horse and foot were to follow in ten days, in order to support Moscow if attacked.

In the morning they took an affectionate leave of each other, and proceeded on their respective routes. Our travellers remained in Petersburgh fourteen days, waiting for a Dutch Galliot, which lay in the Mole at Cronstadt ; and the very day they warped out of the Mole, they heard of the arrival of the Conspirators from Moscow, one hundred and thirty-five in number ; and on their arrival in the Sound at Elsineur, they got a list of the names of those who suffered decapitation, among whom they discovered their landlord—and but fifteen only escaped.

Mr. Wilcox and his company had been three weeks in Amsterdam previous to their arrival, waiting for them, that they might altogether embark for Liverpool. Language, however descriptive, would fall infinitely short of doing justice to this reunion of parties. Love parental, fraternal, filial and conjugal, together with the most unadulterated friendship were interchanged— and the most flattering prospects of approaching happiness, conspired to diffuse a general joy over the whole groupe. Nothing short of celestial bliss could have made any addition to their enjoyments on this occasion —the charms of the ladies seemed to derive new lustre from this change of circumstances and climate—and Captain Wilcox felt the full force of those of Miss Sydney.

Their trip to Liverpool was short, safe and pleasant, and our hero once more set his foot on British ground! in high health, with riches sufficient to support a large

family in the first style of magnificence, for many years,
without any material diminution; for Kerim had made
choice of the most valuable gems in his dominions, be-
sides an immense sum of money, as a token of his respect for him, Charles and Augustus.

Our hero, Charles, Augustus, Eugenio, Mr. Savigny,
Isabella and Terentia, were prevailed on to remain in
Liverpool, until the nuptials of Mr. Cameron with
Miss Wilcox, which was fixed at the distance of two
weeks, and though it appeared an age, yet they could
not refuse to stay; and Captain Wilcox managed
his affairs so prudently, that Miss Sydney gave him
her hand on the same day.

Two days after the celebration of the nuptials, our
hero with all his London friends set out for the metro-
polis, in two post chaises, and George promised to follow in a few days. They had previously committed
a principal part of their treasure to the care of old Mr.
Wilcox, in order to have it remitted to London by the
stage waggon; the remainder, with their wearing apparel
was packed in portmanteaus, and placed behind one of
the carriages, which went foremost, and Eugenio's servant rode behind on the other.

Between Hitchin and Barnet, within nine miles of
the latter, four well dressed horsemen, attended by two
servants in genteel liveries, passed them—they looked

into the carriages as they came alongside, but made no
stop.

Crossing a heath, after sunset, they were alarmed
with the shrieks of women at a distance to the right.
Mercutio immediately proposed going to their relief, his friends agreed, and they jumped out,
drew their swords, and advanced to the spot from
whence the cries proceeded, leaving Mr. Savigny,
Eugenio's servant and the two postillions to guard the
ladies and property. When they arrived at the scene
of action, they found one man engaged at the points
with two, and two ladies weeping, and struggling to
prevent being mounted on horseback, which four men
were striving to effect. Our hero immediately flew to
the assistance of the gentleman, who was wounded in the
sword-arm ; the other three went to relieve the ladies,
whose cries were redoubled when they perceived help
at hand. The ravishers immediately quitted their prey,
and drew to defend themselves. The ladies terrified,
almost to death, placed themselves behind their deliverers, who bore so hard on their antagonists, that three of
them ran off, mounted their horses and disappeared,
leaving their wounded companion grovelling in dust and
blood. Mercutio made short work with his man, having dispatched him the very second thrust, and the old
gentleman had wounded the other so that he could not
make his escape.

Having overthrown this banditti, they had but juſt time to aſk the ladies which way they travelled, when they heard the report of two piſtols, which appeared to them to have been diſcharged where they had left their company and carriages : This threw them into the utmoſt conſternation—they ran precipitately to the ſpot, without ſaying a ſingle word more to the ſtrangers.

It ſeems that very ſoon after they had gone to the relief of the ſtrangers, Eugenio's ſervant, who, as well as the poſtillions, had diſmounted, and while he was diſcourſing with them, obſerved three men carrying off one of the portmanteaus from behind the chaiſe, having cut the ſtraps with which it was faſtened. He ran to his horſe, pulled out his piſtols and diſcharged one of them at the robbers, one of whom dropped, but as he fell, diſcharged his own piſtol at random, which unfortunately killed one of the poſtillions. The other two immediately took to their heels and eſcaped, leaving their booty behind.

Our hero and his companions arrived juſt in time to ſee the portmanteau replaced. The ladies were extremely frightened ; however, as they had received no other damage, the gentlemen re-entered the carriages, and taking the body of the poſtillion, drove on to Barnet as faſt as poſſible—Eugenio's man ſupplying the place of the deceaſed poſtillion.

Although it was late when they reached Barnet, they went immediately before a magistrate, and gave a full and circumstantial account of their evening's adventure: The justice promised to use his utmost endeavors to have the robbers apprehended and brought to punishment.

They staid in town until the postillion was interred, and then set out for London, where they arrived in safety, and put up at the Green Dragon, in Piccadilly, from whence our hero dispatched a porter with a note to his father, (written by Mr. Savigny) as from some friends from Oxfordshire, requesting permission to wait on him in one hour.——The answer was, he should expect them with pleasure.

Mercutio dispatched the carriages, and sent for two hackney coaches, in which they set forward to his father's. They were conducted into a parlour, where they were immediately joined by that gentleman. He thanked them for the honor of the visit, and kindly bid them welcome.

Our hero intended to have kept himself concealed for some time ; but who can withstand the ties of nature ?— filial love, like the overwhelming Nile, bore down every opposing idea. He sprang forward, and, on his knees, clasping those of his father, exclaimed, " Gracious heaven ! do I once more see and embrace my honored father! Behold, your long loft fon!" His father, amazed, raifed and ardently embraced him. "And art thou ftill alive? How has fate confpired to keep thee fo long an exile from thy father's houfe? Oh! Mercutio, your fond mother has never ceafed her lamentations fince the receipt of your letter from Algiers, which is now a long time fince."

Mercutio, in this critical moment, prefented Ifabella as a daughter in-law, and the reft of the company as his moft intimate and fincere friends.

"I am doubly happy this day in the recovery of a long loft fon, the acquifition of a daughter, who would dignify and add fplendor to a throne, and a fet of diftinguifhed friends, with whom, though I have not the honor to be acquainted as yet, I promife myfelf much focial fatisfaction in our future intercourfe."

Our hero anxioufly enquired for his mother, but was informed fhe had left home about two hours before in company with Charlotte Davenport.

"Is my deareft Charlotte well?" interrogated Charles and Auguftus together at the fame time, refpectfully faluting the old gentleman and avowing themfelves.

"My dear friends," faid he, "I am all aftonifhment! She is well—but where, in the name of wonder, or how have you fought out one another? Charlotte

Q   VOL. II.

has been much afflicted—her life indeed was despaired of, when the news from Gibraltar left her no room to doubt of the death of Augustus: This she considered as certain, and expected as a necessary consequence to follow shortly; however, by the tender assiduity of her friends, she is in some measure restored to tranquillity: But your presence will reanimate her, and your endearing caresses will disperse the gloom of melancholy which has long obscured her from the world"——

" But where is she?" hastily interrupted Augustus—" I long to see her—to enfold her in these arms—to reciprocate our past griefs, present joys and future hopes—my dearest Charlotte ! I must see her—where is she ?"

" She went home with Miss Godfrey to Sir Benjamin's, and we will go there immediately. I expect the ladies will all be there."—The chariot being away with them, a servant was dispatched for chairs.

" Well," continued the old gentleman, " the events of yesterday evening were unaccountable; but those of this day are absolutely astonishing."——" Pray, Sir," said Mercutio, " what were those unaccountable events which you mentioned as having taken place yesterday evening ?" " Why," resumed his father, " I took Charlotte and Miss Godfrey, in my phaeton, down to Worley Manor, principally indeed, to divert and amuse the former, where we were induced by the extreme

pleasantness of the weather, and the contemplation of
the variegated and extensive landscape, which, you
know, appears to much greater advantage when op-
posed to the evening ray, to tarry until the sun was near
sitting. About four miles from Worley, we were attacked and surrounded by six Ruffians (Robbers they
were not) well armed and mounted. Two of them
stopped the horses, while two more clapping the points
of their swords to my breast, threatened me with an
instantaneous dispatch, if I only offered the least resist-
ance, or uttered a single word ; and the other two seizing the ladies, forced them out of the carriage—They
shrieked aloud, and struggled to disengage themselves.
The two who were at the horses heads, dismounting,
led their horses in order to assist their companions in
forcing the ladies to mount. Just at this critical instant,
four strangers appeared with drawn swords.

"I had sprang out of the phæton, and was engaged
with the two who had me in charge, and had received
a slight scratch in this arm, when one of the strangers
came to my assistance, who dispatched one of the assas-
sins in a trice, and I wounded the other, I believe, mortally. By this time, the strangers had put three of the
four they were engaged with to flight, the other lay
dead on the field.

"In the moment I was about to thank our deliverers,
we were alarmed by the report of pistols at some distance,
they ran speedily towards the spot, and left us in the

greateſt amazement. And I have ever ſince been in the utmoſt perplexity to account for the ſeveral ſurprizing incidents attending this affair : Without being able to form even a bare conjecture of the cauſe of the attack ; or who the ſtrangers were that flew ſo readily to our affiſtance, and why they left us ſo abruptly on hearing the report of the piſtols : I ſhould certainly have followed them, had not the ladies preſſed me not to leave them ; ſo I ſtept into the carriage, and drove to town as faſt as poſſible."

" Baniſh your ſurprize," ſaid Mercutio, " it was this arm that proſtrated the villain who would have affaffinated my dear father, (of whom I had then not the leaſt recollection)—the other four were defeated by the generous valor of my friends here. We were paffing along the great road towards Barnet, and hearing the cries of the ladies, immediately agreed to go to your relief."

" Miracles ! miracles all !" exclaimed his father, " all bounteous Providence ! Unſearchable are thy ways, gracious God ! But a few hours paſt, my life was expoſed to the greedy ſwords of affaffins—ſuſpended by a ſingle hair over the dreary gulph of death ! Even then, in that critical moment, it was preſerved by a ſon, doubtleſs ſent by Thee, long lamented as dead ; or what would have been infinitely worſe, groaning, expiring daily, under the moſt vindictive torture of Turkiſh bondage. And you, my dear friend," addreffing Au

guftus, " have been highly favored, in being employed
as a guardian angel—in being fent to preferve and pro-
tect the honor of the tendereft, moft faithful of partners,
who is deferving of all your efteem." The arrival of
the chairs interrupted the difcourfe.

Their reception at Sir Benjamin's was fuch as might
have been expected. The furprize, however, which
the fudden appearance of Mercutio and Auguftus infpired, and the want of caution in their introduction,
had like to have been productive of dangerous confequences : The old lady and Charlotte, fwooned in the
fame moment ; however, a few minutes reftored them
to new life—to pleafures to which they had been
long eftranged.

Joy fparkled in every eye prefent—a thoufand ma-
ternal kiffes were impreffed on the lips of his exulting
mother—a thoufand conjugal ones fell to the fhare of
Auguftus, while entranced on the bofom of the enraptured Charlotte. Ifabella was already tenderly embraced as a beloved daughter, by her tender parents,
which rendered her happinefs, as well as that of Mercutio, complete ; and every heart beat in perfect unifon
with thofe immediately concerned.

Dinner interrupted this extatic fcene, after which
Eugenio took leave of his friends, and with Terentia
and Mr. Savigny, fet out for his father's in great George
ftreet ; but before he reached the houfe, the Efcutcheon

Q 2

informed him of his father's deceafe. Auguftus remained at Sir Benjamin's, and Charles returned with Mercutio to his father's.

Our hero's relation of his adventures, which was indifpenfible, occupied moft of the evening—fome parts, for particular reafons (which the reader's reflection will readily difcover) he fuppreffed. His parents were amazed at the ftory, but overjoyed with the refult ; and the fluctuating emotions of their fouls were confpicuous in the changes of their countenances, while he related the various, and to them interefting incidents of which his narrative was compofed.

It is worthy of remark, that though Mercutio's connection with Ifabella, had been fanctioned by a rite of the Church of Rome, which in a Catholic country conftitutes a legal marriage ; yet, as a member of the Church of England, he confidered it in no other light than as a mere efpoufal. He had fome time previous to their marriage, convinced her of the propriety, and apprized her of his intention of keeping feparate beds, until this obftacle could be removed—a line of conduct from which they had never deviated.

Early the next day, our hero accompanied his friend Charles to the houfe of Lord S——, where a fcene fimilar to that exhibited at Sir Benjamin's the preceding day, took place.

The Earl, after listening to Charles's account of their adventures, with profound attention, informed them that the account they had received from their host in Muscow, was in part true; but a great part utterly false. A divorce, he said, had been obtained, but that he was married to the co-partner of his guilt, was a gross falshood invented for the only purpose of concealing a part of that infamy which was stamped on his every action, and which has at last conducted him to an ignominious and untimely death in a foreign land: No, he took her into keeping, and they cohabited some time together, despised by every person of character—no man, but such as were as abandoned as himself, ever entered his house, which was represented as a perfect sink of debauchery, and he, when abroad was shunned as a pestilence. He seduced a young creature, of obscure parents, to his house, where he effected her ruin; however, he had not taken sufficient precaution to elude the vigilance of his paramour: She detected him in the very act, and reproached him in the bitterest terms; accused him of perfidy, and, by a detail of his treatment of herself in particular, enraged the wretch to a degree of madness—he seized a pistol which hung near him, and shot her through the heart. Thus she fell in the prime of life, a victim to the perfidy of a villain and her own levity, weakness and indiscretion—unpitied even by her own father.

His servants, wretches who had been long initiated in the vile practices of their infamous master, were now his only friends and companions ; they affifted him in confining the other unfortunate creature in a dark room, where they left her, then putting horfes to the carriage, and taking as much plate, money and wearing apparel as they thought they could conveniently carry, fet off for Gravefend, where he fold the carriage and horfes, and took fhipping for Ruffia.

Eugenio, Terentia and Mr. Savigny, met them by appointment at Sir Benjamin's, the fame evening, where the two families, with their long loft children, fpent the evening, mutually congratulating each other on the happy viciffitudes which had reftored them to each other, and concluded with adoring and thanking that awful, invifible, yet omnipotent Being, who in mercy had conducted them through that alarming, and to ordinary minds, infurmonntable. dangers and difficulties which we have related, to that haven of felicity and fecurity, in which they had at laft, happily anchored.

Our hero's happinefs was confiderably encreafed that evening, by the appearance of a fifter, who, when he left England, was but nine years of age. He found her in the full bloom of beauty, adorned with every feminine grace. She recollected him in an inftant, exclaimed, Oh my dear brother ! flew to him, and encircling him in the arms of innocence, embraced him with all the ardor of a fond and real fifter.

Charles was deeply smitten with the charms of young Clariffa's perfon and behavior, and determined, if poffible to make her his own. He communicated his fentiments to Mercutio, who approved them and promifed him all the affiftance in his power to procure his happinefs ; nor did he forget his promife, for the very next day he propofed the matter to his father, who returned a favorable anfwer, and Charles was permitted to pay his addreffes to, and foon infpired her with fentiments favorable to his wifhes.

It was agreed between our hero and Eugenio, (who intended to follow his example) to take the earlieft opportunity of having their nuptials re-celebrated. Accordingly a day was appointed at the diftance of fix weeks. This procraftination was jointly concerted between Mercutio, Charles and Auguftus, in hopes Charles's affair would ripen in fuch time, that their happinefs might all commence in one day.

The preffing entreaties of Charles, aided by the perfuafions of Mercutio, and the influence of her parents, at length triumphed over the virgin delicacy of Clariffa : She confented to make him happy on the day appointed for the celebration of her brother's nuptials : She however intreated Charles and Mercutio to have the ceremony performed privately ; but this requeft was over-ruled by the whole family.

The day arrived, they proceeded in coaches to St. James's Church. Their joy on this occasion would have been too exquisite, had not a reflection occurred, which was not conceived till the moment they were advancing towards the sacred altar—which was, that the last time they were assembled in that place, they mournfully assisted at the funeral obsequies of the amiable, much lamented Lucinda, over whose dear remains they then walked in matrimonial procession. Mercutio cast a significant glance at Charles, as if to remind him of their last meeting within those sacred walls ; and as a silent reproach for their inadvertancy in overlooking a circumstance which never could be remembered by them without regret, Charlotte dropt a tear of affection when passing over the ashes of her departed sister. Whatever emotions pervaded their minds while walking from the door to the altar, the most awful, and consequently the most proper behavior was observed through the whole ceremony.

They returned to the house of the Earl of S——, where they dined, in the height of their happiness—genuine felicity pervaded every breast. George Wright and Mr. Cameron were announced. They were introduced by Mercutio, and kindly received. Mrs. Cameron insisted on coming to London, in order to take leave of her earthly redeemer (as she stiled Mercutio) previous to her departure for Scotland, where Mr. Cameron's estate lay.

Having now com,leted my defign, in tracing our hero through the various viciffitudes to which he was fubjected in the courfe of his peregrination, and, finding him at laft, in his native country, furrounded by his moft fincere friends and affectionate relatives, at the very fummit of happinefs, in the poffeffion of the lovely Ifabella, and reinftated in eafe and affluence, I fhall clofe my hiftory.

THE END.

www.ingramcontent.com/pod-product-compliance
Lightning Source LLC
Chambersburg PA
CBHW030600040726
47497CB00008B/2799